DEPRAVITY IN THE DARKNESS

Todd R. Bromley

Copyright © 2023 Todd R. Bromley

All rights reserved.

Editing by KarolynEditsBooks.com

Cover design by fiverr.com/harbingerdesign

TABLE OF CONTENTS

Acknowledgments	i
Preface	iii
Introduction	1
1 | Killers on the Road	5
2 | Madness in the Moonlight	23
3 | On through the Night	37
4 | Run to the Hills	51
5 | Manhunt	63
6 | Statements and Documents	85
Conclusion	123

ACKNOWLEDGMENTS

The materials in this book were derived from interviews with persons directly involved with the case, law enforcement, and official court records. I extend my formal gratitude to residents of Mercer County who endured my numerous queries, requests, and collaborations over the past five years. Particular appreciation is extended to Mercer County District Attorney Pete Acker, whose kindness, generosity, and assistance were invaluable.

PREFACE

With honorable intent, meticulous care, and great detail, the following pages will accurately depict the events that occurred on what one newspaper termed, "The Most Memorable Night of Terror in Pennsylvania's History." Born, raised, and residing in the community where these egregious crimes unfolded, I'm committed to preserving the facts of the horrific events as they transpired. Five years of research and writing were dedicated to this heartfelt endeavor, including historical research, record gathering, countless interviews, and working closely with the Mercer County District Attorney's office.

The extenuating circumstances that caused eight people's lives to violently collide are not lost on me. This unfortunate intersection in life was influenced as much by wealth, class, and opportunity as degradation, depravity, and hopelessness. However, when the sadistic actions of a few affect the lives of many, silence only ensures that future generations will remain ignorant of its truths.

Only God knows a man's heart, but one can safely assume that on a single evening in late March of 1968, the worst that society had to offer forever impacted the best that society had to offer, and for that, we should all be mournful. They were our family, and they were our friends, but nothing would ever be the same again.

INTRODUCTION

Jackson Center sits amid the strip-mined spoil piles and sulfur-tainted streams of western Pennsylvania. The coal-dust-covered hamlet is located some sixty-five miles north of the city of Pittsburgh and twenty-five miles east of the Ohio state line. The township, named after the seventh president of the United States, Andrew Jackson, was founded in 1850. The borough of Jackson Center was established in 1882.

Like most small towns in America post-World War II, Jackson Center endured both the good and the bad times associated with the fluctuating economy of the day. In the late 1960s, its population neared 300, and many of the area's working-age men sought out the higher-paying steel mill and factory jobs located to the south, while a smattering of locals persevered by scratching out a seasonal living through farming or working for a nearby road-grading company.

Even though one of the county's only railroad switches was located near its boundary and a new interstate highway that would pass by its doorstep was under construction, Jackson Center was rarely the destination of those seeking the

American dream. Even at its peak, a significant percentage of the local population fell below the national poverty level, and for most of the young men in the area, Vietnam or a less-than-desirable labor job loomed large in their immediate futures. A town known for having more bars than any other public establishments overwhelmingly produced hard-working, hard-drinking, blue-collar men.

Sixty-two miles southeast of Jackson Center and nearly a world away, Ford City is located along the east bank of the Allegheny River. Founded in 1887 as a company town by the Pittsburgh Plate Glass Company, the city was named after the company founder, John Ford. The factory itself employed as many as 5,000 workers during its heyday, and in the late 1960s, Ford City's bustling population exceeded 4,000 residents.

As the city of Pittsburgh exploded economically and expanded during the steel boom, money, jobs, and prosperity spilled into the surrounding areas. Financial institutes, colleges, hospitals, and highways presented avenues of opportunity never previously available to the area's working class. Ford City was one such beneficiary, and if you lived within the bubble of the steel city, the future appeared to be quite bright with endless possibilities.

As the winds of change swept across the nation in the late 1960s, western Pennsylvanians were mostly immune to much of the nonsense that was transpiring elsewhere in the country. There were no communists, hippies, or anti-war protesters there. Just hard-working Americans that went to work every day, paid their taxes, and were quite content to exist in their ordinary lives.

That is, until the evening of March 28, 1968, when some of those lives collided and something went horribly wrong.

1

KILLERS ON THE ROAD

Until one morning in late March of 1968, few Americans—in fact, few Pennsylvanians—had ever heard of Jackson Center. The slumbering borough had remained exempt from exceptional incidents since its founding, which suited the residents just fine. The majority of them survived from paycheck to paycheck. Still, these unpretentious citizens were quite efficient out of necessity at supplementing their resources through various means, such as gardening, hunting, fishing, and trapping. Community ties were generational, and no one was a stranger. Nearly every residence harbored at least one firearm, and locking your doors would be considered an insult to the neighbors. Except for an occasional scuffle at one of the local beer gardens, there was no crime or threatening menaces to cause concern.

Daily adventures for prepubescent children growing up in the area rivaled those of Huck Finn and a care in the world they did not have. However, as youths progressed through their teenage years, minimal outlets for alleviating the angst associated with restless adolescence existed. Due to the area's low census numbers, all school-aged students were bused some seven miles north to the Lakeview Area School District, which encompassed the majority of townships and small boroughs located in the northern part of Mercer County. The student body was a consistent mixture of town and country youths with zero ethnic diversity.

An unfortunate byproduct of the region's socioeconomic landscape was an unusually high dropout rate among high-school-aged males, which only added to the clouded social dynamic in an area that was already lacking. Any semblance of teenage gatherings outside the framework of academic extracurricular activities typically occurred in the form of weekend beer parties at one of the numerous abandoned strip mines in the area.

The only prominent architectural structure in Jackson Center sat squarely in the middle of town and was a beacon for those who chose to partake in regulative worship. The venerable two-story Presbyterian church was one of the few places where husbands and wives could socialize communally. For the most part, due to organizational social segregation, the local women could be found spending their spare time at the grange hall or playing bingo at the volunteer fire company while the men folk tarried away their free time at the sportsman's club or one of several bars.

As the world tuned into the nightly news in late March, they were informed that a major offensive in Vietnam had finally come to an end but any expectations that the war was close to ending were shattered by the announcement that President Johnson would not be running for re-election later that fall. A noteworthy news event, to be certain, but for the residents of Jackson Center, it would pale in comparison to the horrifying headlines that would be bestowed upon them in the morning. Putting it all behind them would take the shattered community decades.

/////////

Spring came earlier than usual for western Pennsylvanians in 1968, with temperatures reaching twenty degrees above average. As the Allegheny River wound its way past the occupants of Ford City, the dogwoods and daffodils along its banks were already in full bloom. Ever the quintessential American melting pot, Ford City drew in workers and their families from over thirty-five identifiable ethnic backgrounds, and the glass they produced at the local Pittsburgh Plate Glass Company touched every skyscraper in the United States.

The city's own infrastructure exhibited the same quality and attention to detail. Block after block of well-manicured row-style houses and immaculately kept business fronts inadvertently displayed the wealth flowing through the community. The city's vast array of churches were architectural marvels in their own right and represented the strength and fortitude of its vibrant populous.

The community offered a sparse suburban feel and contained many public attributes associated with economic resourcefulness. There was no need to leave the city limits to fulfill any personal need or sustain one's livelihood. Those seeking cultural refinement could easily do so by making the short drive into Pittsburgh. If you were transitioning from high school to adulthood, college was most likely in your future, along with the endless opportunities that higher education presented.

As part of the Armstrong Public School District, Ford City was home to its own elementary school, junior-senior high school, and the area's only Catholic school. The Ford City High School basketball team energized and seemingly profited the life of the entire city. Businesses proudly displayed their support in storefront windows, and on game nights, all seats in the gymnasium were filled, and for good reason. Winning the section title was an annual event and over the years, the teams amassed a Western Pennsylvania Interscholastic Athletic

League record of thirty-four section titles. Every garage in the city was said to have a basketball hoop attached to it, and citizens were quite proud of their young athletes.

Kenneth Michael Frick, aka Mike or Big Mike as his closest friends called him, was a native son of Ford City and was, by all accounts, going places in life. At an impressive six feet, three inches and 245 pounds, he was a standout high school athlete in multiple sports and a member of his student council and the National Honor Society. At an age and size that would've made many adolescents uncomfortable with their inability to blend in, Mike could be characterized as easygoing, confident, and reliable. He was very much liked by both his teachers and his peers.

During his senior year of high school, Mike attracted the attention of several Division I colleges and accepted a full athletic basketball scholarship to the Virginia Military Institute (VMI). Mike entered VMI as a civil engineering major and was a member of the Newman Club and the American Society of Civil Engineers. In addition to being a two-sport collegiate athlete (baseball and basketball), Cadet Frick was also a Dean's List student who coached a high school league basketball team in his spare time.

The middle child of three, Mike and his siblings—an older brother and younger sister—were blessed with a stable home life and loving parents who instilled in them virtuous morals.

Under the tutelage of this staunch Catholic upbringing and four disciplined years at one of the country's most prestigious military institutes, Mike was a well-polished young man who took pride in his appearance and actions. His attention to detail was meticulous from his well-kept hair, horn-rimmed glasses, tucked-in shirt, and belt-cinched pants.

With only weeks remaining until he graduated from VMI, Mike was offered an engineering position at the Bethlehem Steel Corporation and granted a Dean's List furlough to visit home one last time before commencement. All the hard work and commitment were finally coming to fruition for the twenty-one-year-old. When a close friend asked him to join in on a double date on the evening of March 28, 1968, Mike accepted the invitation.

/////////

That same afternoon, some sixty-two miles to the northwest, twenty-one-year-old Kenneth Eugene Perrine, aka Kenny, was sitting on a bar stool at the public drinking establishment known as Herron's, located on the east end of Jackson Center. He was a handsome cut of a man with dark eyes and swept-back, jet-black hair accompanied by long sideburns that personified his bad-boy demeanor. He was a likable enough fellow at first impression, but no one ever knew which Kenny they were dealing with at any given moment.

He was mostly a braggart but would not hesitate to throw down with anyone as if he had something to prove.

Kenny was the third youngest of ten children. From an early age, he demonstrated a very low tolerance for authority and concealed a great deal of repressed hostility that would frequently lead to him acting out with aggression. He dropped out of high school in the ninth grade, and psychological testing indicated that he possessed very low intelligence and poor planning ability. He would later be diagnosed as a psychopathic sociopath, but it was during his teenage years that he developed a very low opinion of himself and an extremely pessimistic attitude concerning the outcome of his life in general. These perceptions climaxed at the age of sixteen when he tried to commit suicide by shooting himself in the chest. Surviving this attempt on his own life, he began to display the pattern of living that would continue to characterize him up to the present time.

Married in January 1966, Kenny had a one-year-old and two-year-old at home with a third child on the way. Despite the young man's many problems and faults, he undoubtedly was the best version of himself in the presence of his family and had a genuine concern for their well-being. He loved his children to the best of his capabilities, but throughout his marriage, he struggled to find and maintain a job for an extended period of time.

During his short marriage, he squandered employment opportunities at a railroad steel car plant, a service station, and most notably, the highway department in Jackson Center, which would play a pivotal role in the events that would transpire later in the evening. Because of his inability to maintain employment coupled with an abundance of tedious, unproductive downtime, Kenny could not financially provide for his family, which brought on clinical bouts of depression. During these inactive periods, his demons would come calling.

On July 5, 1966, only seven months into his marriage, Kenny was drinking heavily at Jack's Place, located in Jackson Center on the corner of State Routes 62 and 965. After the last call, he inconspicuously followed an inebriated acquaintance home from the bar until they reached a driveway on the outskirts of town. When the man opened the driver's door, Kenny pulled him from the car, beat him nearly unconscious, robbed him of his wallet, and sped away. Taking an indirect route to discard the wallet and driving some fifteen miles to the neighboring community of Mercer, he then robbed the local VFW bar of an undisclosed amount of cash and liquor.

Kenny was identified as the perpetrator of the crimes and was later sentenced to twenty-four months in the Allegheny County Workhouse. Like most people with similar natures, he found tolerating the frustrations of incarceration difficult.

During his time in prison, he developed an addiction to barbiturates that would plague him for the rest of his life.

Paroled for his crimes in November 1967, fourteen months into the sentence, Kenny Perrine was back out in society, a convicted felon with no source of income and a severe drug addiction. Between November 1967 and January 1968, he would be arrested several more times and indicted on rape, robbery, and burglary charges.

As he sat in Herron's bar on March 28, 1968, popping pills and drinking draft beers, he was set to stand trial the following week for the aforementioned robbery and burglary charges.

Sitting alongside Kenny was twenty-seven-year-old Donald Russell Hosack, aka Donnie, or as Kenny often called him, Midget. Standing barely five feet tall, Donnie was a most deplorable individual who exhibited every known trait associated with "little man syndrome." Born in Mercer County, his parents divorced when Donnie was five, and he moved with his father to Michigan. Under the guidance of his father, he was taught the finer intricacies of becoming a thief, and his father would send him out several times a week to ply his trade.

He was eventually removed from his father's custody at age fourteen because of his escalating juvenile delinquent behavior and sent back to Mercer County to live with his mother and her new husband. He was enrolled in Mercer Area High School but dropped out in the tenth grade. The change of living venue had no lasting effect on Donnie, and his downward spiral continued until he was placed in the SCI Camp Hill Reformatory in Cumberland County, Pennsylvania. A psychological evaluation revealed that Donnie was naturally a follower with very low intelligence and already demonstrated an alcohol abuse pattern.

Upon his release from the reformatory, he once again took up residence in Mercer County and found steady employment at a dairy farm. He was married in the summer of 1962, moved his young bride to Slippery Rock and began working for the Miller McKnight Coal Company north of Jackson Center. The union produced a son and a daughter, but the marriage began to develop problems with reports of infidelity and domestic abuse attributed to Donnie's heavy drinking. The couple separated twice, once in 1965 and again in 1966.

During their second separation, Donald Hosack and accomplice Gary Batley—Kenny Perrine's half-brother—abducted a thirteen-year-old Mercer area girl while she was walking home from school and drove her to some isolated railroad tracks on the outskirts of town, where they both proceeded to rape her. After the pair finished the deed, they kept their young victim in the vehicle for several hours, threatening her and her family with bodily harm if she ever spoke of the incident to anyone. Eventually, after they released the terrified minor, she immediately told her parents of the horrific ordeal. Hosack and Batley were both arrested and charged with rape.

At the time of the incident, Batley was a minor, and the rape was adjudicated as a juvenile offense. Hosack, while awaiting trial on the rape indictment, was again arrested for assault and battery and was also the main suspect in an armed robbery in a neighboring county. Not waiting for a jury of his peers to decide his fate, he jumped bail.

As Donnie Hosack sat in Herron's bar this warm, sunny afternoon, he was a wanted man on the run. A third individual, Arthur Paul McConnell, or Art as he was known to everyone, had driven Hosack and Kenny Perrine to the bar. The previous day, Art had rented a blue 1968 Ford sedan from Robbins Motors in Mercer, and the trio arrived at Herron's bar shortly after noon. Concealed inside the vehicle were three firearms: a .22-caliber Revelation rifle, a .22-caliber Winchester rifle, and a 20-gauge pump shotgun.

Art was several years older than his companions and quite the enigma in comparison. Until this point in his life, the thirty-seven-year-old had been a regularly contributing member of society. Born and raised in Mercer County, he was the youngest of five, a high school graduate, and had served two years in the United States Marine Corps before being honorably discharged.

Just before Christmas 1955, Art married Sarah Batley, the aunt of Gary Batley—Kenny Perrine's half-brother and Donnie Hosack's accomplice in the rape of the young girl. By all accounts, Sarah was the center of Art's world, and they endeavored to build a happy life together. Art was employed at Shenango Furnace, and the couple purchased their first house in 1957. A reliable worker who never drank alcohol and was never heard uttering a single cuss word in the presence of his coworkers, Art was well-mannered and appeared to have his life on track. That is, until Sarah was diagnosed with aggressive stage four cancer in 1965.

Art stayed by his wife's side through the entire ordeal, seeking religious counseling and the best medical care he could afford, but before the year was out, Sarah succumbed to her illness. Art was devastated. Now a man seemingly without a focus, he began to drink heavily, was laid off from his job, and fell behind on his mortgage. On this day, like so many other days over the past year, Art sat in a bar drinking himself into oblivion.

After spending the afternoon at Herron's bar, Perrine, the group's shot caller, decided it was time for the trio to seek out some excitement elsewhere. He ordered a six-pack of Koehler cans for the road then jumped behind the wheel of the blue Ford at 5:00 p.m. and sped off toward the borough of Mercer. Up to this point, their day had consisted of drinking draft beers combined with Perrine's continuous consumption of barbiturates. They'd traveled less than half a mile when the trio spotted a familiar face standing in front of the Texaco gas station. Perrine wheeled the car into the parking lot, bringing it to a screeching halt. Holding up a can of beer, he asked, "Hey, little brother. You want to go have some fun?"

Nineteen-year-old Gary Batley was a mentally challenged young man who idolized his older half-brother. Gary had been a special-education student in the Lakeview area school system and flunked both first and second grades before dropping out of school entirely in the eighth grade. Evaluated at the level of functioning illiterate, Gary was easily confused, manipulated, and coerced.

Already a convicted rapist by the age of nineteen, he'd never held any employment for more than two weeks and spent most of his days wandering around town, hoping to secure some form of illegal narcotics, which he ingested daily when available. This day was no different; he'd been getting high for most of it. When the opportunity to "have some fun" presented itself, Gary eagerly accepted the invitation and got into the vehicle.

In addition to the three firearms, the rental car now contained four drug- and alcohol-impaired individuals who, on their best days, could not make good life decisions. Three of them had previously been arrested for rape, prison was awaiting one upon capture, one would most likely be sent back to prison the following week, and another felt like he'd lost everything in his life worth living for. As the blue Ford headed out of Jackson Center carrying this cataclysmic combination of depravity, no one yet knew what the evening had in store.

Bypassing Mercer, Perrine, McConnell, Hosack, and Batley arrived at the Traditions bar located on State Route 58 at 5:20 p.m. Eager to take their all-day drinking up a notch, everyone but Hosack entered the bar and ordered double shots of Seagram's Seven and grapefruit. Hosack, who had previously been banned from entering the establishment, remained in the backseat of the blue Ford and continued drinking beer alone in the parking lot.

As the evening passed, the three inside the bar continued to drink whiskey, and Perrine took more barbiturates, now sharing them with his half-brother Batley. Occasionally, someone would take a quart of Koehler's beer out to Hosack and talk with him for a while, but for the most part, the trio remained inside, mingling among the other patrons. After spending the past three and a half hours drinking whiskey, Perrine again decided it was time to head down the highway and rallied his cohorts to the rental car.

No one was more excited to leave the premises than Hosack, who'd been confined inside the automobile since they'd arrived. With eight hours of drinking beer and whiskey under their belts, coupled with Perrine's and Batley's heavy drug intake, Perrine, sitting behind the wheel, asked, "Where to, boys?" Hosack, who resided in the Slippery Rock area, spoke up, claiming to know of a fun place near his home, so at 8:45 p.m., the blue Ford headed to the Coat of Arms roadhouse.

//////////

At nearly 7:00 p.m., Mike arrived in the family station wagon to pick up his good friend, Rick. The rendezvous time had been established earlier in the day when Rick made arrangements with his girlfriend Jean, a twenty-one-year-old senior at Slippery Rock University, to secure a friend for a double date with Mike later that evening. Jean's close friend and nineteen-year-old dormmate Kathy was a sophomore at the university and, having briefly met Mike once, agreed to the date and sharing in the night's activities. As it was a Thursday evening and classes were scheduled in the morning, the young coeds planned on making an early evening of it.

As Mike and Rick pulled onto the 422 interchanges on the outskirts of Ford City and headed west towards the city of Butler and then on to Slippery Rock, the sun was starting to set in front of them on this unseasonably warm spring day. With great anticipation, the pair made good time and arrived at Slippery Rock University's North Hall dormitory slightly before 8:00 p.m.

Even though they were ready when they were notified that their dates had arrived in the lobby, ever-refined young ladies Jean and Kathy elected not to present themselves until shortly after eight, the prearranged scheduled date time. The two couples made small talk in the lobby until Kathy realized she'd forgotten her transistor radio and went to her room to retrieve it. When she returned to the lobby, they stepped out into the evening, with Rick and Jean getting into the station wagon's back seat as Mike and Kathy got into the front seat.

As the couples drove into the town of Slippery Rock, they discussed going to see a movie but then realized that everyone had already seen the movie that was showing. So, after riding around town for a bit, the decision was made to go and buy some beer. Arriving at the Springs Tavern located on State Route 8, Rick, Jean, and Kathy remained in the car while Mike went inside and purchased two four-packs of Budweiser. Upon his return, the girls stated they knew of a quiet, out-of-the-way place where fraternities sometimes gathered to drink and dance. The small establishment was located on the outskirts of town, so they drove back into Slippery Rock and arrived at the Coat of Arms shortly after 9:00 p.m.

The Coat of Arms was located in a desolate area at the end of a dirt lane off the main highway. Upon arrival, the couples were discouraged to find that it was already closed for the evening. Still, because of its seclusion, they thought it an excellent place to finish drinking the beer they'd purchased and engage in small talk. Mike swung the car around in the parking area, pointed it towards the dirt lane that led to the highway, and shut it off.

The new Otis Redding song, "Sittin' on the Dock of the Bay," which the girls had never heard before, was playing on the radio as Mike and Rick carried on a lively discussion about who had the better wristwatch. Mike had recently purchased a Speidel-banded Benrus wristwatch with see-in-the-dark technology. He was proudly showing it off to all of them at 9:20 p.m. when they noticed headlights coming down the lane toward them.

2

MADNESS IN THE MOONLIGHT

The blue Ford rolled slowly past the parked coeds to the front entrance of the Coat of Arms. Its occupants were not dissuaded by it being closed and saw it as an opportunity to burglarize the establishment. Perrine backed up along the side of the building so the front of the car was facing the dirt lane that led to the highway and he would be able to keep an eye on the back of the parked station wagon, which sat directly across the parking lot.

Hosack and Batley got out of the car and went around to the back of the building to see if they could gain entry. Noticing what they perceived as an active burglar alarm, they retreated to the car and reported it to the others. Calmly sitting behind the wheel smoking a cigarette, Perrine pointed to the parked station wagon in front of them and said, "We need to get whoever is in that car into this car."

In his rearview mirror, Mike watched the blue Ford maneuver around the parking lot and then back in along the side of the building. Thinking it was some teenagers parking, he joked about it to the others. While sitting in the front seat with Mike, Kathy turned to get a better view and stated that she could see doors opening and closing on the car. All was still for the next five minutes, then suddenly, the blue Ford came forward at high speed, stopping within inches of their rear bumper, and its headlights began flashing.

Initially, the coeds weren't overly alarmed, thinking it was only kids messing around. Still, when the headlights continued flashing for several minutes, they felt it was in their best interests to vacate the premises. When Mike started the station wagon, the blue Ford backed up and hastily swung around the passenger side, stopping nearly broadside in front of them. Kathy yelled for Mike to "get out of here," but at her urgent request, the blue Ford's doors swung open, and for the first time, the coeds got a look at the individuals inside.

Springing from the vehicle, Perrine approached the driver's side of the station wagon. Pointing his rifle directly at Mike's head and tapping its barrel on the window, he commanded, "You boys, get out of the car!" Simultaneously, McConnell and Hosack approached the passenger side of the vehicle with their weapons at the ready. Mike exited the front driver's side of the station wagon where Perrine and Batley were now positioned, and Rick exited the back passenger side where McConnell and Hosack were positioned. Mike and Rick were ordered to produce their wallets and were then escorted at gunpoint to the front of the car.

Kathy and Jean were still sitting inside the station wagon when Hosack and Batley directed their attention toward them. By this point, Jean was starting to break down, and she reached up from the backseat and clasped Kathy's shoulders with her trembling hands. Hosack, pointing his rifle at her, told her, "Get out of the car," as Batley pulled Kathy across the front seat and out the driver's door. Both girls were led to the front of the vehicle with the others and told to place their hands on the hood and to keep them there.

Perrine, opening the trunk of the blue Ford, leveled his rifle at Mike, and ordered him into it. Protesting profusely, Mike finally submitted to the demand and climbed into the trunk lying lengthwise with his head on the vehicle's passenger side. Next, Rick was ordered into the trunk with his head on the driver's side. The trunk was then closed, and Perrine told the others that the big guy was going to be a problem.

Kathy and Jean were told to remove their hands from the hood of the station wagon, at which time Perrine told Batley to "pop the hood." Opening it, Perrine ripped out the vehicle's electrical harness and cast it into the parking lot. After closing the hood, he ordered Jean into the back seat of their car between McConnell and Hosack and forced Kathy into the front seat between Batley and himself. Exiting the dirt lane at a high rate of speed and leaving the Coat of Arms in their dust, the blue Ford and all eight occupants were headed back to Jackson Center.

///////////

Only minutes into the abduction, Mike and Rick desperately searched for a way to escape the trunk. Neither of them were able to find a release latch, so they simultaneously tried to push the trunk lid open to no avail. Hearing their commotion, Hosack yelled to them from the backseat, "Knock it off, or I'll shoot you right through the seat!"

Perrine again admonished, "The big guy is going to be a problem."

As they raced down the highway at speeds reaching ninety miles per hour, Kathy nervously watched the speedometer as her four abductors passed around the firearms inside the vehicle along with cans of beer. No one was saying much, and she thought it odd that the man to her right, Batley, was wearing sunglasses when it was dark outside. Sitting in the backseat, Jean kept her gaze focused on the floor, desperately trying to keep her emotions intact.

Once Jean and Kathy were forced into the blue Ford, they were in unfamiliar territory. Traveling on a seemingly endless maze of dirt roads at high rates of speed only added to their confusion. Finally mustering up the courage, Kathy asked, "Where are we going?"

Perrine responded with, "Are you scared?" When she replied that she was, Perrine laughed and told her they'd just robbed a bank in Kentucky.

Batley propped up the 20-gauge shotgun that was between his legs and, caressing it, said, "This is old faithful. We been through a lot together." He and Perrine then erupted into laughter.

Perrine directed his next question to the backseat and asked Jean, "How much money have you seen at one time in your life?"

Jean answered, "Not too much." McConnell, sitting next to her, produced a roll of small bills from his pocket and fanned them out. Jean nervously said, "That doesn't look like too much."

Perrine laughed again, saying, "Well, little brother, I guess they're onto us. Now we'll have to tell them the truth."

Batley then proceeded to inform the girls that they were in a motorcycle gang and that they were taking them back to their clubhouse to ride motorcycles together. He also claimed that they liked playing chicken on their motorcycles and that Kathy would be riding with him.

Perrine, seemingly agitated by this statement, said, "I told you she's going to ride with me." Then, directing his attention to Kathy, he said, "That's how it is with us. If you want something, you have to fight for it." Kathy, very confused by the entire exchange, thought they were complete idiots, but knowing she was in a dangerous situation, remained silent.

Retracing their earlier route and heading back toward the Mercer area on State Route 58, Perrine pulled into Brownie's bar at 10:15 p.m. No other vehicles were in the parking lot, so he pulled up close to the entrance and shut the car off. Hosack yelled back to Mike and Rick asking them if they were alright. Mike replied that they could use some air. Hosack told him to shut up and then told Perrine that the big guy was causing trouble. Perrine called McConnell out of the car for a quick conversation, then went into the bar and returned with two six-packs of Black Label and two packs of cigarettes. Squealing the tires as they exited the parking lot, the blue Ford was again back on the highway.

/////////

After a short distance, they turned off the blacktop onto another dirt road and traveled at a much slower pace. Jean and Kathy, still in somewhat of a state of shock and bewilderment, began to collect their wits enough to consciously start remembering road signs and other landmarks that they passed.

Perrine stopped the blue Ford near a small, dilapidated house on Oakland Road, and McConnell got out. Perrine continued down the dirt road until it reached a tee where it met a blacktop road. He then turned the car around and slowly headed back in the direction they'd come from. As they approached the area where McConnell had exited the vehicle, Kathy could see him kneeling in the weeds along the side of the road. Perrine again stopped the car, and McConnell returned to the back seat, but he now had two blankets in his possession.

Continuing down the dirt road to its end and turning left, Perrine again brought the car to a halt and backed it into a dark pull-off area adjacent to some railroad tracks. As he shut the car off, it was now 10:30 p.m. Opening another can of beer and lighting a cigarette, Perrine rummaged through his pockets for the bottle of pills. When he'd begun his ingestion of the barbiturates some ten hours earlier, the bottle held well over fifty capsules. Less than half that amount remained, as Batley had consumed his fair share as well, and now Hosack began to partake in the drug use. By sunrise, the bottle would only contain six capsules.

Mike and Rick had been inside the trunk for an hour, and the accelerated backroad, cross-country ride had not been pleasant. After Perrine finished his cigarette, he thought it was time to give the "boys in the back" some air. He summoned McConnell with his rifle to the rear of the car and told the others to stay in the car. Perrine opened the trunk and announced to Mike and Rick it was time for a boxing lesson. In his narcissistic, braggadocio fashion, he stated, "I've been in Vietnam, and I'm going to show you a thing or two." Nothing could have been further from the truth. Perrine didn't have the mental fortitude to endure the Boy Scouts of America, let alone the United States Armed Forces. Under the protection of McConnell's rifle, he ordered Rick out of the trunk.

Slightly disoriented and with unsteady legs, Rick attempted to crawl from the trunk into the refreshing night air. When his first foot hit the ground, Perrine punched him in the face and then twice in the stomach. With his other leg still hung up inside the trunk, Rick doubled over and began to lose his balance as Perrine pushed him back into the trunk and slammed its lid.

Laughing about what had just happened, Perrine took the rifle from McConnell, retrieved a blanket from the back seat, and then ordered Kathy out of the car at gunpoint. Once outside the vehicle, Perrine put the blanket over her head and twisted it tight. Then pulling her by the blanket as if she were on a leash, he led her toward the railroad tracks. Tripping and stumbling after a short distance, Kathy started pleading with Perrine to remove the blanket from her head.

When they reached the railroad tracks, Perrine finally agreed to remove the blanket if she promised to forget that she'd ever seen the area. Kathy was willing to say anything to have the blanket removed and agreed. Perrine pulled the blanket from her head but informed her that she had to carry it, and they continued down the tracks. Not feeling overly confident about the outcome of her situation, Kathy hesitantly asked, "Where are we going?"

Perrine responded, "To our clubhouse. This is all just part of an initiation for our motorcycle club. The guys bet us that we wouldn't do this, so all we have to do is take you up there and show you to them, and then we can let you go."

Continuing down the railroad tracks a bit farther but with the Ford's interior light still in view, Perrine ordered Kathy to cross over the railroad siding and into the woods. After walking only a few feet, he told her to spread the blanket on the ground. Confused by the order, Kathy did as she was told, asking, "Why?"

Perrine pointed his rifle at her and said, "Shut up and take off all of your clothes except for your blouse." Kathy, sobbing and pleading with Perrine not to do this to her, removed her clothes from the waist down. Perrine leaned the rifle against a tree, removed all his clothes, and then directed his attention to Kathy's blouse and bra, which he slowly removed. Once he had her completely undressed, he forced her onto the blanket and proceeded to rape her.

When he was done, they both got dressed and Perrine ordered Kathy to pick up the blanket and head back down to the railroad tracks. They had yet to take a step when they noticed someone holding a flashlight coming down the railroad tracks toward them. Perrine pushed the rifle barrel against the back of Kathy's head and told her, "Don't move and keep your mouth shut." As the light drew closer, Kathy recognized one of the two people as Jean by her white jacket. When she relayed to Perrine that it was only Jean, he retorted, "Shut up!"

Holding a flashlight in her right hand, Jean was being escorted down the railroad tracks by Hosack, who had a rifle pointed at her back. Hosack continued a short distance past Perrine and Kathy, unaware that they were there, and then ordered Jean to the side of the railroad tracks. Removing his shirt and laying it on the ground, he ordered Jean to remove her clothes from the waist down and put her ass on the shirt. Jean, whose mental state had been slipping since the abduction, was starting to crack emotionally. She followed his commands then Hosack dropped his pants to his ankles and began raping her.

After Hosack and Jean had walked past them, Perrine again ordered Kathy to head back to the blue Ford. Upon reaching the car, he shoved Kathy over to McConnell and said, "It's your turn." Grabbing Kathy by the arm, McConnell led her back to the railroad tracks and Perrine and Batley followed them.

Once again pleading for this not to happen, Kathy asked McConnell, "Why are you doing this to me?"

He stated, "If you was me, you'd be doing it too. I don't have no college education, no nice house, no nice car, and no nice wife. I don't have anything, so if you was in my shoes, you'd be doing it too."

Hearing Jean crying in the darkness somewhere in front of them, McConnell ordered Kathy in that direction and told her to spread the blanket down within a few feet of where Hosack had just finished raping Jean. McConnell next made Kathy remove her pants and underwear, pushed her down onto the blanket, and began raping her while Perrine kept the rifle barrel hovering just inches above her face. Hosack and Batley illuminated Kathy's torture with their flashlights.

After McConnell's assault, it was Batley's turn with Kathy while Perrine simultaneously raped Jean. As Kathy's horrific ordeal unfolded with Batley on top of her, she could hear Perrine telling Jean that she'd better open her legs, or he was going to start shooting her toes off. As the double rape progressed, McConnell and Hosack laughed and made derogatory comments while directing their flashlights back and forth between the assaults.

After the atrocities were completed, the four criminals stood around cracking jokes and smoking cigarettes as Kathy, now on her hands and knees, tried to find her clothes while Jean incoherently hummed and rocked back and forth just a few feet away.

After finishing their cigarettes, the criminals escorted the girls back down the railroad tracks at gunpoint, but the assaults hadn't yet concluded. Upon reaching the vehicle, cans of beer were passed around, and then Hosack again demanded that Kathy spread the blanket out on the ground next to the car and remove all of her clothes. Hosack then raped her in the presence of the others as Batley forced Jean into the back seat of the blue Ford and raped her. Once Batley had finished his assault, McConnell then took his turn with Jean in the back seat.

As McConnell and Batley's assault on Jean took place in the back seat, for the first time, Mike and Rick could hear the torture the girls were enduring. As the violence continued only inches away, they had no way to stop the brutality. Over the sound of Jean's audible suffering, Mike pounded on the trunk lid, hurling expletives at his abductors. They did not penetrate the unconscionable minds of the perpetrators, but Perrine once again stated that something had to be done about the big guy. Jean and Kathy had both been raped four times—once by each of their abductors.

/////////

At 12:30 a.m., Perrine ordered everyone to return to their same positions in the blue Ford, and they were again on the road. At this point, Mike and Rick had been locked in the trunk for over three hours, except for the thirty-second beatdown Rick had sustained. Jean and Kathy were scratched, bruised, and emotionally spent from the viciousness they'd endured but were vigilantly trying to remain conscious of their surroundings for future reference. Their captors, seemingly having the time of their lives, continued drinking, smoking, popping pills, and telling jokes. Hosack continued to tell the same Jack and Jill joke throughout the night ad nauseam.

However, twelve hours into this drug-infused and alcohol-intoxicated day, Perrine had come to his own mental crossroads. Tormented by the fact that he would be returned to prison in just days on the prior burglary indictments, he was trying to determine how far he was willing to take this crime spree. With an IQ of only eighty, he'd made a lifelong habit of surrounding himself with those who were even less intelligent. This served several purposes, but mainly made him feel superior. In his grandiose, tough-guy fashion, he liked to be the leader and shot caller, as evidenced by the day's events. Although he considered McConnell and Hosack friends, and Batley was his younger half-brother, he cared little about any of them and didn't feel any loyalty to them. His only motivation was furthering his own agenda—everyone else was expendable.

Although he'd never indicated signs of organic brain disease, hallucinations, or psychotic breaks, he was diagnosed early on with poor planning abilities, impulsive disorders, and a low tolerance for frustrations. No reasonable person would choose these attributes in a leader and adding drugs and alcohol to the equation made for a volatile brain cocktail. His degenerate cohorts couldn't possibly have seen this concoction stirring, but it would have made little difference if they had. They lacked the mental capacity to comprehend anything beyond their immediate deviated pleasure.

As if suddenly awakened to this fleeting moment of reality, Perrine convinced himself that the only viable options were to persuade the captives to keep their mouths shut or ride this thing into the depths of hell and never return from its abyss. Nothing was more telling of this significant moment of doubt when he solemnly asked both Jean and Kathy, "If we give you five hundred dollars and let all of you go, would you be willing to forget this whole thing ever happened?" Neither of the girls replied. The damage had already been done.

Unbeknownst to everyone else on this hellacious ride, a critical turning point was reached in this pivotal instance. And unfortunately for its passengers, the same person driving the blue Ford was also driving the events that would forever shape the rest of their lives. And he was about to carry them past the point of no return.

3

ON THROUGH THE NIGHT

As the blue Ford raced towards Jackson Center, for the first time, Jean and Kathy spotted what would become their north star and a beacon of light. Rising one hundred feet above the Foster Grading Company building was a radio tower, topped with a red pulsing light. Over the next several hours, regardless of how far they traveled or how many back roads were traversed, that light would always be in their view. The unknown area suddenly no longer contained the same vastness it once did, and the girls were determined to try and mentally document where they were in relation to the red light.

Mike and Rick were starting to feel the effects of being enclosed in such a confined space for so many hours and were desperate for relief. Their bodies were cramping in the hot, dark trunk full of exhaust fumes, especially because they had been rolled to and fro at accelerated backroad speeds. Mike, who was not a small man, yelled and pleaded for those inside the car to let them out for some air. Hosack relayed to Perrine that the big guy was again causing trouble, and McConnell immediately requested that the radio volume be turned up. Fully back from his momentary lapse of humanity, Perrine turned up the radio and stated, "I've had about enough of the big guy." Mercy was not one of the qualities these criminals possessed.

Passing directly by the radio tower, Perrine wheeled the car onto the next dirt road to the left, and as it fishtailed up the slight grade, Kathy memorized the road sign, N. Foster. For all the trauma and terror they'd endured over the past three hours, the girls, now in survival mode, were amazingly aware of their surroundings, knowing their lives possibly depended on it. Traveling less than a mile up the road, Perrine slid the car into a small parking area with a sign that read "Pennsylvania Department of Highways - Jackson Center."

The Jackson Center division was nothing more than a parking area with a small metal shed nearby. A few rolls of snow fence were stacked on the premises, along with a pile of leftover cinders from the winter's road maintenance. Occasionally, the county's road grader would be stored in the lot, but for the most part, it served as the rendezvous point for its six employees. The small shed contained various hand tools used by the work crew and a small amount of cash in the event urgent repairs or gas was needed.

Perrine, previously an employee of the Jackson Center Highway Department for a very short time, was quite aware of what the shed contained, and that's what he was there for. Removing a tire iron from under the driver's seat, he exited the car and attempted to pry the lock from the shed. After several failed attempts, McConnell left the vehicle to assist him. Still having little success, the two spied a long pipe next to the shed and were able to leverage it enough to break the clasp partway from the door.

With McConnell pulling back the bottom half of the door, Perrine was able to worm his way inside the shed. Knowing where the cash box was hidden, he quickly commandeered the ten dollars it contained and then started looking for what he'd come for. After a few minutes of scanning the shed's contents with his flashlight, he located two long-handled shovels and passed them through the door to McConnell. Both men returned to the blue Ford, and McConnell placed the shovels on the floor of the back seat with their handles propped against the rear driver's side door. A moment later, they were again in motion as Perrine tore out of the parking lot.

////////////

The countryside surrounding the Jackson Center borough was a heavily coal-mined region. One could stand in the center of town and view the strip-mined wastelands and towering spoil piles in all directions. Coal dust would blow in with the wind, and the sweet aroma of burning coal wafting through the streets could be smelled during the winter months as coal silt settled upon the residential rooftops. At the east end of town stood a large coal tipple that would fill the dozens of passing railroad cars twice daily. The grid of temporary parking areas, lanes, and excavation roads that led to and from the mines were too numerous to label.

The criminals were very familiar with the area's ever-changing landscape. Perrine, driving toward the Jackson Center borough, turned onto a side road to avoid entering the town, continued for a short distance, and turned onto what the locals called "Skunk Lane." Skunk Lane was nothing more than a muddy two-track that wound its way through unclaimed spoil piles to access the back recesses of the still-active strip mine. The local adolescents also used the area as a lover's lane parking spot and occasionally to host beer parties. All of the criminals had previously been down the lane.

As the blue Ford turned into Skunk Lane, the pulsating red light was directly in front of them, so Kathy knew they hadn't traveled far. She also noticed a woody hillside to her left, and as they continued further down the lane, they came upon a large piece of equipment. With panic again setting in, Jean began sobbing, and Kathy urgently demanded to know why they were going back down this lane. The only response she received came from Hosack, who told her, "Shut up!"

Coming to a wider pull-off area, Perrine turned the blue Ford around, pointed it back down the lane in the direction they'd just come, and shut it off. Opening another can of beer, he told McConnell to "grab the shovels." At this point, Jean lost it, and Kathy pleadingly explained there was no reason to kill them. Perrine ordered Hosack into the front seat to guard Kathy and told Batley to stay in the backseat with Jean.

After Perrine and McConnell carried the shovels into the darkness, Hosack again raped Kathy, and Batley raped Jean. By this point, the girls were physically and emotionally spent, having both been raped five times. As the latest assaults concluded, Jean incessantly moaned in agony from the back seat, which infuriated Hosack, who threatened to shoot her if she didn't shut up.

Perrine and McConnell walked about one hundred feet and stopped to discuss their next course of action. From the time of the abduction, Perrine had been concerned about Mike's intimidating size and build, fearing if the situation ever led to a physical altercation, Mike could probably handle each of them in short order. McConnell agreed, and then Perrine added, "If we kill one of them, we have to kill them all." Perrine was not ready to part with the girls yet, so it was decided that Mike and Rick would be killed now, and the girls would be eliminated later after they had more fun with them.

Finishing his cigarette and setting his beer on the ground, Perrine began to dig Mike and Rick's graves. McConnell joined in, but immediately the two had to change plans. Because of the mining that had taken place in the area, digging was nearly impossible. The hard pan and shale were almost impenetrable, and Perrine and McConnell weren't the most energetic individuals to ever wield a shovel. After thirty minutes, they'd roughly carved out a twenty-inch-deep indentation into the ground and decided that would have to do for the time being. They agreed the grave would suffice for the big guy, and they would relocate to kill the others.

It was now 1:00 am, and Mike and Rick had been locked in the trunk for nearly four hours. Upon returning to the car, Perrine ordered Hosack out of the front seat and told him to bring his rifle. He then told McConnell to get in the front seat with Kathy and turn the radio up. Moving to the car's rear, Perrine opened the trunk and said, "Get out!" Rick started to climb out but was told to stay in the trunk and that the big guy was the only one they wanted. Mike was now free of the trunk for the first time since this night of terror had begun. He was ordered to walk up the lane into the darkness; and told that if he didn't cause any trouble, he would be tied up where the mine workers could find him in the morning.

As Mike was removed from the trunk, Kathy and Jean knew something was happening at the back of the car. Facing the opposite direction and cloaked in darkness with the radio's volume turned up, they could feel the car moving up and down as if someone was climbing out of it. They assumed the boys were being taken from the trunk but could not confirm their suspicions because as Mike was escorted up the lane, McConnell pushed Kathy down onto the front seat and raped her for the sixth time. Batley, emotionally charged by what was going on in the front seat, began to molest Jean again but could not complete the rape because he could not achieve another erection.

After the short walk into the darkness, Mike was ordered to stop and put his hands behind his back. Unbeknownst to him, he stood less than ten feet from his grave. Perrine, in a true cowardly fashion, lacking the fortitude to commit to the occasion, put his rifle to the back of Hosack's head and said, "Shoot him, or I'll shoot you." At approximately 1:10 a.m. on the morning on March 29, 1968, Donald Russell Hosack, under the direction of Kenneth Eugene Perrine, shot Mike in the back of the head with a .22-caliber Revelation rifle.

After crumpling to the ground, Perrine and Hosack drug Mike's lifeless body to the shallow grave, laying him face up with his head to the north. Before the loosened shale and coal dust were spread atop him, Perrine removed the Speidel-banded Benrus wristwatch that Mike had been so proud of just four hours earlier and placed it on his own wrist. Later autopsy reports revealed that the bullet penetrated the posterior surface of the neck between the occipital protuberance and the base of the neck and lodged in Mike's left cheekbone. An even more disturbing find was that the wound was not immediately fatal, and Mike lived for an additional ten minutes after being buried alive.

Returning to the car, Perrine opened the trunk, threw the shovels on top of Rick, and quickly closed it again. He ordered McConnell and Batley from the vehicle to update them about what had just transpired and to keep their stories in line, then it was decided that the girls would be told that Mike was tied up and would be left in the area. Jean and Kathy were doing their best to collaborate on a plan of action, but Jean was again struggling and in a very fragile emotional state. When the criminals returned to the car, they noticed a missing firearm. Panicking and blaming the girls, they discovered after a quick search that Hosack had left it lying outside the car. With all weapons accounted for, the blue Ford exited Skunk Lane, and the torturous ride into madness continued.

///////////

Only traveling a short distance, Perrine once again wheeled the car into a strip-mined area near the area they'd just vacated. The criminals, demonstrating their level of intelligence, chose another nearly identical strip mine with the same hard pan and shale surface to dig their next grave in. Perrine ordered all the criminals from the car and removed the shovels from the trunk, instructing McConnell and Batley to go dig the grave. When completed, they would be tasked with removing Rick from the trunk, walking him to the grave, and then shooting him. This way, all of the conspirators would have blood on their hands, Perrine explained.

Returning to the car, Perrine and Hosack opened another beer, popped more barbiturates, lit cigarettes, and spun the tale to the girls that Mike had been tied up and left in the area they'd just vacated and would be found in a few hours when the mining crews arrived for work. For McConnell and Batley, things went awry from the start. Batley refused to dig because the ground was too hard and stated, "I ain't gonna kill nobody."

McConnell called him a "chicken shit" and said he would dig the grave and do the deed alone. Several minutes later, having only scratched out a small area a few inches deep, McConnell gave up on the digging, and he and Batley argued their way back to the others.

Upon reaching the car, McConnell chastised Batley and told Perrine, "He's nothing but a coward and a chicken. He's not going to do it!" Perrine, agitated by the unfolding events, threw the shovels back in the trunk on top of Rick and ordered the others into the car. By this point, Rick was seriously worried. Smelling and feeling the fresh coal residue on the shovels and knowing Mike hadn't returned to the car, he started to fear the worst. And for the first time, he could make out their abductors' conversation as they argued with raised voices. The thought that one of them was calling the other a chicken caused him great concern for his well-being.

Perrine started the car, ripped it into drive, and bounced out of the strip mine at a high rate of speed. Now headed north past Jack's Tavern onto State Route 62 and directly past his mother's and Batley's father's house, he was headed for the softer soiled agricultural areas north of Jackson Center. As they continued traveling at an excessive speed, Kathy could see the pulsing red light in the distance off to her left. Enraged that McConnell and Batley hadn't followed his orders, Perrine violently slid the car off the highway onto another dirt road, and something on the blue Ford broke.

The time was now 2:15 a.m., and the criminals were in a precarious position. Pushing the car onto a tractor path concealed from the dirt road, Perrine ordered Batley into the front seat to guard Kathy and told Hosack to stay in the back seat with Jean. Next, he informed McConnell that the two of them would walk back to his mother's house and try to secure another vehicle, and then they disappeared into the night. Hosack and Batley took to immediately raping the girls again. At this point, Batley had somehow convinced himself that Kathy was in love with him and told her they would escape from the others and run away together.

Perrine and McConnell arrived at his mother's residence at 3:00 a.m. After waking his mother and stepfather, he asked and was granted permission to use their telephone. Perrine promptly called his wife, who was pregnant and had two toddlers at home, and told her to bring the automobile containing his tools to his mother's house. His wife delivered the 1960 Ford Galaxie at 3:30 a.m. Leaving his wife at the Batley residence, he and McConnell immediately drove the Galaxie back to where the broken-down blue Ford was hidden.

Batley, who was still plotting his escape with Kathy, assured her that Mike was safe and tied up back at Skunk Lane and that he would take care of Hosack, let the other boy out of the trunk, and then they could run across the fields to his house. Those plans were dashed as headlights turned onto the tractor path, bringing them all back to the reality of the moment. Perrine, retrieving his toolbox from the trunk of the Galaxie, told the others to get out of the blue Ford. He then ordered Batley into the Galaxie and told him to keep guard over the girls while the others repaired the car. Rick knew that something was wrong with the car, but he was never removed from the trunk. Within thirty minutes, the criminals had the blue Ford repaired, and they were back on the road shortly after 4:00 a.m.

////////////

As if the evening's events hadn't already been terrifyingly bizarre, they were about to get even stranger. Having lost a combined three hours trying to dig through the second strip mine's hard pan surface and fixing the broken-down blue Ford, Rick's murder was again put on hold. Perrine ordered McConnell to drive the blue Ford and take Jean and Batley with him while he climbed behind the wheel of the Galaxie, with Kathy and Hosack as his passengers. Incredulously, as if they were some pretentious teenagers without a care in the world, the two drivers played a high-speed game of tag on the dirt roads surrounding Jackson Center for the next hour.

The criminals seemed oblivious to the consequences of kidnapping, rape, and murder as they whooped it up, hollering at one another as the cars would pass or race side by side. In the process, Rick was severely battered and rolled around inside the trunk, but the girls regained their mental composure. They took this opportunity to remember the license plate numbers on each vehicle as they passed one another. They were also both quite aware of the pulsing red light that was sometimes close and sometimes in the distance but always visible.

The four perpetrators would occasionally stop to parlay with one another or shoot at deer that were spotted close to the road, but the fun and games once again suddenly ceased when McConnell got the blue Ford stuck. Perrine ordered Hosack out of the car to help the others get it unstuck. Keeping Kathy with him in the Galaxie, he kept circling the area, hoping to prevent another passerby from happening upon them.

With daylight fast approaching and morning traffic beginning to pick up, they were finally able to free the blue Ford. Perrine ordered Kathy out of the Galaxie and into the other vehicle with everyone else, and they followed him back to his mother's place to return the car. Instead of pulling into the driveway, McConnell edged the blue Ford off to the right-hand shoulder of the road. Still sitting in the front seat, Jean clearly made out the name BATLEY on the mailbox.

Batley retrieved mail from the box, placed it inside the vehicle's glove box, and proudly exclaimed to Kathy, "This is my house." Having previously only heard their abductors' first names, the girls now also knew Gary's last name. Perrine, rejoining the occupants of the blue Ford, climbed into the back seat, and once again, the criminals were in motion.

4

RUN TO THE HILLS

As McConnell drove the blue Ford out of Jackson Center, streaks of daylight began to pierce the eastern horizon. Jean and Kathy could see the pulsing red light off in the distance to their right, and then suddenly, it was gone from view. The atmosphere inside the car had turned somber, and the criminals' storytelling, laughing, yelling, and joking had ceased. Exhaustion and mental fatigue were setting in as the effects of the drugs, alcohol, and evening's events were wearing on the criminals.

At a little past 5:30 a.m., McConnell turned into the driveway of a run-down house that Kathy instantly recognized as the same house that Perrine had let McConnell out at almost seven hours earlier. Pulling the car around to the back of the residence, McConnell gathered the blankets from the blue Ford, took a key from his pocket, and unlocked the door of the badly dilapidated structure. Perrine ordered the girls out of the car and into the house. They were directed to the living room, where Kathy was told to sit in a chair, and Jean was made to sit on a tattered blanket-covered sofa.

As Perrine, Hosack, and Batley lingered near the girls, McConnell went upstairs and returned carrying wire and binder twine. Perrine, telling Batley to guard the girls, directed McConnell and Hosack to join him outside. Still convinced that Kathy was in love with him, Batley again promised the girls that he would help them escape. He would need a little time to determine Perrine's plan, and then he would figure out a course of action. Although Jean and Kathy considered Batley mentally slow, he seemed to be the most compassionate of their abductors. However, they had little faith in his desire or ability to help them. After all, he'd been an active participant throughout the evening and had raped them both. Still, with little other hope, they told him they would follow his lead when the time arrived.

Rick, who'd been trapped inside the trunk for over seven hours and was completely unaware that he'd narrowly escaped death on three separate occasions was now ordered from the trunk and told to put his hands behind his back. McConnell then took the binder twine, tied Rick's hands, and pushed him toward the house. With a gun barrel in the middle of his back, he was ordered up the stairs to a bedroom and told to lie face down on the bed. Taking the wire provided by McConnell, Perrine pulled Rick's left leg up towards his back, wrapped one end around his ankle, and then tied the other around his neck. Pleased with their handy work, Perrine and McConnell quietly discussed their intentions for the captives and then rejoined the others downstairs.

Telling everyone to get some sleep, Perrine ordered Kathy to join him in an adjacent bedroom while Hosack lay down on the couch with Jean, and McConnell settled into the chair vacated by Kathy. Still pacing about carrying the 20-gauge shotgun, Batley was working himself into a nervous breakdown wanting nothing more than to go home. Tired and spent, reality had come full circle for him, and he knew they'd committed many unforgivable acts. He could hear Perrine raping Kathy in the next room, and as she endured her eighth assault, Jean lay weeping on the couch.

Sensing Batley's torment, McConnell pulled him aside to calm his nerves and told him, "Relax. Everything will be fine. We're going to kill them all as soon as we get some rest, and no one will ever find out." That wasn't the assurance Batley was hoping for. He told McConnell he wanted to get some sleep and joined Rick upstairs.

From the instant he was left alone, Rick began to pick at the binder twine that bound his hands. He wasn't sure what type of material he was tied with, but it felt like it could be separated if he slowly worked at it. While trying to free himself, Batley entered the room and saw what he was attempting to accomplish. He confirmed to Rick that his efforts were working and that he should continue trying to get free. He also stated, "These guys are crazy. They are going to kill all of you." He then told him that he would help him and the girls escape when the time was right.

After Perrine finished raping Kathy, he left the bedroom and found McConnell asleep in the chair. Prodding him awake, Perrine told him it was his turn and pointed to the bedroom where Kathy was still lying naked on the bed. McConnell climbed into the bed with her but did not assault her and instead fell fast asleep, as did Kathy. Perrine, succumbing to exhaustion, fell asleep in the chair as Hosack and Jean dozed off on the couch. For the first time since the perpetual onslaught of depravity had begun, all was still.

///////////

At 9:30 a.m., twelve hours into the abduction, the criminals once again began to stir. First, Batley and then the others started to awaken from their short slumber. Still lying naked on the bed, Kathy asked permission to get dressed and use the bathroom. Perrine, granting her request, summoned the rest of the cohorts outside for a briefing of the morning's plans. Knowing of a secluded spot in the Pardoe area approximately five miles away, he and McConnell would drive the blue Ford there and dig a mass grave. Hosack and Batley were charged with keeping guard over the captives until their return when they would all accompany their victims back to the grave, shoot, and bury them. With Perrine's plan laid out, all of the criminals went back into the house and, with the exception of Batley, began their morning by doing shots of whiskey followed by a few beers. Perrine and Hosack finished the remaining barbiturates as they prepared for the morning activities.

Rick had finally managed to untie his hands from behind his back and remove the wire from his neck and ankle and was now desperately trying to find a way to escape while the downstairs remained quiet. Removing the window and frame adjacent to the bed, he spied an antenna pole within easy reach. Starting to exit the bedroom through the window, he suddenly heard footsteps coming up the stairs. As he quickly retreated to the bed, Batley entered the room and saw what he was attempting. Assuring Rick that the time was not right, Batley told him that two of the guys would be leaving soon and would be gone for about an hour. Once they left, he would bring the two girls upstairs, and while he distracted Hosack, the three of them could climb down the pole and make their getaway together. However, Batley stressed that Rick needed to appear tied up while in the presence of the others. Directing him back to the window, he pointed in the distance and said, "Run to the hills. Just on the other side is Mercer. You'll be safe there."

As Perrine and McConnell prepared to leave on their grave-digging excursion, panic quickly ensued when a red and white 1968 Chevy pulled into the driveway. Perrine, ordering McConnell and Hosack to cover the girls' mouths, threatened to shoot anyone who made a sound. Positioning himself next to the door with the 20-gauge shotgun, Perrine nervously watched as a middle-aged man wearing a three-piece suit, hat, and carrying a case approached the door. Completely unaware of the imminent danger, the man knocked as Perrine leveled the shotgun at his head only inches away. After several tense minutes, the man returned to his car and left the property. Breathing a sigh of relief, Perrine turned to the others and said, "Fucking salesmen."

With the disastrous interruption averted, the mornings' plans were back on track. Perrine noticed that Hosack was already visibly impaired from his morning drug and alcohol intake and admonished him to stay alert then told Batley not to let the girls out of his sight or answer the door for anyone. Throwing the shotgun on the front seat of the blue Ford between McConnell and himself, the two left to prepare Rick, Jean, and Kathy's graves.

//////////

When Perrine and McConnell left, Batley summoned Kathy to the bedroom. She joined him, thinking they were about to plan their escape. She spotted a pocketknife lying on the floor next to the bed. Apparently, it had fallen from McConnell's pocket while he was asleep in the room earlier. Batley picked up the knife and put it in his pocket. Kathy sat on the edge of the bed, anxiously awaiting her escape instructions, when Batley said, "Take off all of your clothes."

In utter shock and disbelief, Kathy broke down crying and said, "I thought you were going to help us?" After removing his pants and pressing against her, Batley again told her to remove her clothes. Kathy screamed for him to get away and yelled, "Can't you tell when a person has just had enough."

As she tried to fight him off, Batley knocked her back onto the bed. Sobbing uncontrollably, Kathy tried desperately to get out from underneath him. This only enraged Batley, who retrieved the rifle he'd placed by the bedroom door, put it to her head, and said, "Take off your clothes or die." Fearing for her life, Kathy did as she was told and was then raped for the ninth time.

Hosack was passed out in the chair in the next room, and Jean was sound asleep on the couch. Rick, still upstairs, knew that the blue Ford had left and was awaiting his instructions from Batley when he heard Kathy's most recent assault taking place. After the rape, both Batley and Kathy got dressed, and Batley held out the pocketknife and told Kathy he was going to give it to the boy upstairs. He then told Kathy to go upstairs, and that he would send Jean up to join them, then they could make their getaway.

Kathy went upstairs and was surprised to find Rick sitting on the bed untied. After unsuccessfully trying to awaken Jean, Batley came up the stairs and told them that Jean wouldn't wake up. As he handed Rick the pocketknife, he told him that he would instead try to get Hosack upstairs, at which time they could jump him and escape. Not believing a word that he was saying, Kathy remained seated on the bed, weeping as Rick tried to decide whether to overtake Batley, who was still wielding a rifle, or let the morning's events unfold on their own.

Suddenly, Jean let out a blood-curdling scream and came running up the stairs exclaiming, "He's trying to rape me again." Jean huddled with Kathy on the edge of the bed while Rick opened the pocketknife and leaned back on his arms, pretending to still be tied.

Hosack slowly climbed the stairs with a rifle in one hand and a can of beer in the other. As Hosack approached the top step, Batley asked the girls if they wanted anything to drink. Kathy replied that she did, and as Hosack entered, he looked at Batley and said, "Why? They're all dead anyway."

Batley retreated down the stairs as Hosack, clearly intoxicated, slowly and deliberately pointed his rifle at each of his captives' heads and, with slurred words, said, "Maybe we'll just hang you all now instead of waiting for the others to get back." After returning with a can of 7UP, Batley handed it to Kathy, who immediately poured it into a heavy mug sitting atop a wooden box at the end of the bed. She then placed the empty can on the floor. For the first time, all of the house's occupants were together in the same room.

Knowing that Hosack's rifle was missing its clip and could only hold a single bullet at a time, Batley attempted to get him to fire it by pointing out a small pill bottle sitting on a ceiling rafter across the room. Betting Hosack that he couldn't hit it, the challenge was not accepted, so Batley raised his rifle and shot at it. Missing the bottle, Batley tried to goad Hosack into shooting at it again. Hosack continued balking at the idea, so Batley fired at it again. Hosack, not taking the bait, called Batley a dumbass for shooting inside the house. Batley stated that he needed some fresh air, walked down the stairs, out the door, and did not return.

Not realizing that Batley had wholly abandoned the premises and was headed home or that Rick's hands were no longer tied, and he was now armed, Hosack continued to taunt his captives verbally. Waiting for their opportunity to pounce, the three captives intently watched his every move. Finally, when he staggered too close to the bed and removed his hand from the trigger to rub his eyes, the moment they were anticipating was at hand. Jean lunged for the barrel of the rifle, grabbing it with both hands as Kathy threw her 7UP into Hosack's eyes and began beating him about the head with the heavy mug. Rick sprang from the bed, stabbed him twice in the torso, and then pushed him to the floor, smashing the window he'd previously removed and rested against the wall.

At the sound of the breaking glass, Jean rushed down the stairs, still carrying the rifle, with Rick following. Hosack, trying to get up from the floor, managed to grab Kathy from behind, but she was able to break free of his grasp as he once again tumbled to the floor. Now running for their lives, they headed out of the house as fast as their legs could carry them and up the hill in the direction Batley had told them to flee. As they neared the top of the hill, Jean handed Rick the rifle as they waited for Kathy to catch up. Before Kathy reached them, they saw Hosack in the distance pointing his rifle in their direction as the blue Ford pulled into the driveway. Continuing their run to freedom, the trio crested the top of the hill to see the towering sphere of the Mercer County Courthouse and the entire city of Mercer before them, only a few hundred yards away.

/////////

As Perrine and McConnell pulled into the driveway, they saw Hosack running out of the house with the front of his shirt saturated in blood. Instantly, they believed he'd been shot, but as he ran around the side of the house, they looked in the distance just in time to see Kathy running over the hill. Perrine screamed at Hosack for letting the captives escape, knowing it would be futile to try and go after them. Hosack frantically explained that Batley had untied the guy upstairs and abandoned him, causing him to nearly get killed. With time now working against them, the criminals gathered the firearms, alcohol, and a few essentials from the house before they attempted to put as much distance between themselves and Mercer as possible. With Hosack bleeding profusely in the back seat, Perrine avoided the main highways and headed east.

Holding onto each other's hands, the coeds ran, stumbled, and tumbled down the hill towards a road cutting through the countryside. As they neared a barbed-wire fence, Rick threw the rifle into some high weeds and assisted the girls in navigating the fence. Back on their course to freedom, they could see a rural-mail vehicle coming down the road. Running as fast as they could to intercept the vehicle, they arrived at the roadside, exhausted and out of breath as the vehicle approached.

As the mail carrier slowed to a stop, Kathy frantically asked the female driver if she would be passing by a police station. Looking a little bewildered, the mail carrier stated, "There isn't a police station anywhere around here." Kathy then anxiously asked if any of the houses in the area had a telephone. Pointing to a house about a quarter of a mile down the road, the mail carrier said, "I know that house has a phone. They'll be able to help you." Wishing them good luck, she then drove away.

Continuing their run down the road, the exhausted trio continued looking behind them, dreading the appearance of the blue Ford. Finally, they reached the house, ran onto the porch, and began to pound on the door hysterically. An older woman cracked the door, and Kathy, entirely out of breath at this point, tried to explain that they would like to use her telephone. Nervously sizing up the tattered trio, the elderly woman stated, "I don't have a phone. You'll have to try somewhere else," and promptly closed the door.

With desperation setting in and not knowing which direction to go, Rick, Jean, and Kathy dejectedly started back towards the road when a young woman carrying a basket of clothes came around the side of the house. Kathy immediately asked her if she had a telephone they could use. The woman said they did, invited them into the home, and pointed out the phone. The older woman who had denied them permission was sitting on a couch across the room and was visibly upset by their presence. At 10:50 a.m. on the morning of March 29, over thirteen hours into their abduction, Rick dialed the operator who connected him with the Mercer County State Police.

5

MANHUNT

As the blue Ford headed out of Mercer County, its occupants believed they could escape capture if they lay low for a few days and then left Pennsylvania entirely. Ironically, had they initially driven west when fleeing, within thirty minutes they could've crossed the Ohio state line and been deep into the Midwest long before law enforcement was even aware of the full scope of their crimes. By heading in the wrong direction, they gifted their pursuers time critical to organizing early on in the investigation.

Completely underestimating the size of the manhunt about to be brought down upon them, the criminals plotted their revenge on Batley and discussed their next course of action. McConnell devised a plan to hide at a remote hunting camp in the wilderness area of Tionesta, located over an hour east of where their egregious crimes were committed. Having previously been to the area with a former coworker, he convinced the others it would be an excellent place to hole up for a few days. With the plan set in motion, their first order of business was to fill the car with gas and secure some type of medical attention for Hosack, who was bleeding from his stab wounds. Abandoning their back road escape strategy, they drove into the city of Franklin.

Hosack remained in the back seat because he was covered in blood, and had McConnell purchase basic medical supplies at a storefront drug store while Perrine gassed up the car and sought out a payphone. Making contact with a friend in the Jackson Center area, Perrine reported that he and his cohorts were running from the law and would need money and assistance getting out of the state. This new conspirator agreed to help the criminals when they were ready to move. Perrine rendezvoused with and relayed to the others that they had an accomplice back home willing to help them evade capture then drove farther away from civilization and into the seclusion of Pennsylvania's wilderness region.

After traveling for thirty minutes, Perrine stopped at a roadside general store. He and McConnell entered the store and were met by a bubbly young blonde-haired woman who asked them if she could help them find anything, where they were from, and what they were doing in the area. Not giving them a chance to reply, she said she saw few strangers this time of the year. Perrine ignored her onslaught of questions, but McConnell answered, saying, "We're just passing through on our way to do some fishing." After purchasing food, drinks, tobacco, and rolling papers, they were quickly back on the road.

Eventually finding a remote cabin in a region that seemed void of human activity, the criminals cased it out and then kicked in the door to gain entry. With limited furniture, and no electricity or running water, it wasn't much, but it would do for the time being. Searching through the contents of the cabin, they found a 12-gauge single-shot shotgun, a box of shotgun slugs, and a flashlight. Perrine and McConnell unloaded the alcohol, firearms, and recently purchased items from the blue Ford and settled in for their long day of solitude. Hosack, still complaining about Batley, cleaned and bandaged his wounds.

/////////

On the Friday morning of March 29, the telephone rang early and often at the Mercer County State Police barracks. Shortly after 7:00 a.m., they received their first call from the Jackson Center Highway Department supervisor reporting a tool shed burglary. At 8:40 a.m., the Butler County State Police called to report that four people had gone missing from the Slippery Rock area and were seeking assistance with their investigation. At 10:50 a.m., Rick made the call that would eventually tie all of the crimes together.

At 11:10 a.m., Trooper William Mifsud of the Mercer County State Police was dispatched to the address on Home Street where Rick, Jean, and Kathy anxiously awaited his arrival. Immediately placing them in his patrol car, it was apparent to the experienced officer that the trio had endured and survived a horrific ordeal. The only questions he asked them while they were en route to the police station were concerns directly related to their physical well-being.

Arriving at the station within minutes, the coeds were provided with linens and directed to washrooms so they could clean up. After being offered something to eat and drink, each was asked to give an individual statement concerning the abduction and the events that had transpired after they were abducted. Their statements were recorded and transcribed, and each victim signed and dated their statement. When this was completed, the coeds called their parents, and police personnel contacted Mike's parents. At 11:45 a.m., Jean and Kathy were transported to Bashline Hospital in Grove City for medical examinations.

While giving their statements, Jean and Kathy stated they only knew their abductors by their first names—Ken, Art, Don, and Gary—but both had seen the mailbox with "Batley" on it, and Gary had stated that it was his house. They had also memorized the license plate numbers of both vehicles. Kathy recited the blue Ford's plate number as "3A3 222," and Jean reported the Ford Galaxie's number as "R09 392." An officer immediately ran the plate numbers through Pennsylvania's

Registrations Bulletins. The blue Ford was returned as owned by Robbins Motors of Mercer, who rented the vehicle to Art McConnell. The owner of the Galaxie came back as Kenny Perrine's mother-in-law. Although at this time no physical evidence linked Hosack to the crimes, from the coeds' descriptions, the name (Don) they'd heard his cohorts call him, and his prior criminal association with Batley, the police were confident they had identified all four perpetrators. At 11:50 a.m., exactly one hour to the minute from the time that Rick had made contact with the police, a teletype went out across the state of Pennsylvania.

> All-Points Bulletin 287: MERCER COUNTY: WANTED FOR KIDNAPPING AND RAPE: ARTHER PAUL MCCONNELL-AGE 37: DONALD RUSSELL HOSACK-AGE 27: KENNETH EUGENE PERRINE-AGE 21: GARY LEE BATLEY-AGE 19: MAY BE TRAVELING TOGETHER: LAST SEEN IN A 1968 BLUE FORD SEDAN: REGISTRATION NO. 3A3222: SHOULD BE CONSIDERED ARMED AND DANGEROUS.

After completing his statement, Rick was asked to help identify the house where he had reportedly stabbed one of the criminals. After reviewing the rescue location of the coeds, troopers were certain the dwelling was located on Oakland Road. The first order of business was to see if the person that Rick had stabbed was alive or needed medical attention. Rick accompanied two officers to McConnell's residence and immediately recognized the dilapidated house. There was no sign of anyone at the home, however, the blood-covered pocket-knife was still lying on the bedroom floor. A search warrant would need to be obtained before any evidence could be gathered from the premises, so they returned to the police station to contact the district attorney.

Simultaneously, the search for Mike, who they believed to be alive and tied up in the Jackson Center area, was underway. Knowing this was an extraordinary situation and that every attempt must be made to find both Mike and the criminals, every Mercer County state trooper was contacted and told to report for duty immediately. Ten additional officers and five cars were brought in from the Butler County State Police barracks along with state police air support. With over fifty state police officers involved and local law enforcement from numerous surrounding municipalities conducting road checks, the second largest manhunt in Pennsylvania history was launched in and around Jackson Center.

//////////

Jean and Kathy arrived at Bashline Hospital at 12:00 p.m. The examinations revealed both girls had spermatozoa in their vaginal secretions along with vaginal tearing. Both had been bitten, scratched, and bruised but had sustained no life-threatening physical injuries. While their examinations were in process, the parents of both girls arrived at the hospital. Upon discharge, Jean and Kathy were transported back to the police station with their parents in tow. At 12:45 p.m., the girls agreed to voluntarily accompany officers in an attempt to retrace their route from the previous evening with the hope of finding where Mike had been left tied up. As the patrol car, with both girls riding in the back seat, pulled out of the police station, Mike's parents pulled in.

Traveling down Oakland Road, the girls observed a significant police presence around the house where they had been held captive just hours earlier. Having obtained the search warrant, police and forensic crews were now actively combing the entire area. Accompanied by troopers, Rick led them up the hill behind the house to the barbed-wire fence where he'd disposed of the rifle. The .22-caliber Revelation rifle was recovered, photographed, and turned over to the evidence team.

The officers accompanying Jean and Kathy continued the slow grid-like searching pattern, systematically navigating every back road, hoping the girls would recognize something. Finally, Kathy spotted the railroad grading where the first assaults had taken place, and both girls escorted the officers down the railroad tracks to the exact locations the rapes had occurred. The area was located on what locals called "Dump Road." The girls were placed back into the police car so officers could continue searching for Mike while other officers searched the new crime scene. Evidence found, labeled, and secured included three cigarette butts, two unspent .22-caliber shells, and a quarter.

The next area the girls recognized was the Pizor strip mine just north of the Springfield Church on the Jackson Center/Grove City Road. Jean and Kathy were always inside the blue Ford when they'd been in this area, but they were sure it was the right location. When the officers quickly scanned the area, they discovered two sets of foot tracks traveling in both directions on the lane. Radioing for assistance, they moved on with the girls as other officers searched the area and found the two sets of foot tracks, freshly matted-down grass, and a newly dug area that measured three by five feet and six inches deep.

Continuing their cross-country search, the girls spotted the pulsing red light on the radio tower above the Foster Grading Company. Kathy pointed out the tower and said, "We have to be getting close to where Mike is now." With great anticipation, everyone in the patrol car became keenly alert. The next recognizable waypoint was the Batley residence. Jean and Kathy excitedly exclaimed, "That's Gary's house!" The state police, having already unsuccessfully attempted to locate Batley at the home, documented Jean and Kathy's identification of the Batley residence and continued with the search.

At 5:00 p.m., the last discovery the girls were able to make was the tool shed that the criminals had broken into on North Foster Road. Having searched for four hours, they could not locate the areas where the blue Ford had broken down or where Mike was taken from the trunk. Discouraged, tired, and hungry, they were returned to the police station to eat, spend time with their parents, and get some rest before making another attempt to find Mike. All of the other resources and manpower activated to locate Mike were unsuccessful as well.

As the manhunt neared its ninth hour and darkness settled in, nearly twenty hours had passed since Mike had last been seen. The coeds, their parents, and Mike's parents comforted one another at the police station as the minutes tortuously turned into hours. The first break in the case occurred at 8:45 p.m. when the 1960 Ford Galaxie registered to Kenny Perrine's mother-in-law was discovered in a Mercer County apartment complex. Breathing some hope into the investigation, Jean and Kathy were taken to identify the car. Upon confirmation that the vehicle was indeed the one Perrine had forced Kathy into earlier, events now began to unfold rapidly.

At 9:10 p.m., the decision was made to split the girls up and place them in separate patrol cars so more territory could be covered. The officers' hope was that with the red pulsing tower light clearly visible in the night sky, one of the girls may be able to gauge the direction and distance needed to locate Mike.

They both confirmed that the tower light was close and clearly visible when Mike was removed from the trunk. Twenty minutes into their latest search efforts, all state police personnel in the vicinity of the Jackson Center area received a radio transmission to immediately report to the Winklevoss service station located on the west end of town and await further instructions.

///////////

As the day tediously progressed for the criminals, they were already becoming restless. Entirely out of barbiturates and nearly out of alcohol, they argued among themselves and cursed Batley for their current predicament. Hosack, finally getting the bleeding from his wounds under control, felt much better but feared he would need medical attention soon. Perrine, desperately wanting to find out what was happening back in Jackson Center, suggested they try and locate a pay phone but was talked out of it by McConnell. For the time being, the criminals would remain at the cabin.

For the residents of Jackson Center, their entire world had been turned upside down, and it didn't appear that things would return to normal anytime soon. With a massive police presence throughout the area, in addition to checkpoints and the continual overhead air surveillance, word of what had transpired while they slept began to spread through the community. Rumors began circulating that Perrine, Hosack, and Batley were the perpetrators of the crimes. Supposing the criminals were most likely still among them, most residents welcomed the chance to eliminate them. Although many residents locked their doors and windows for the first time in their lives, the male populous was not afraid of the young hoodlums, and most possessed the shoot-on-sight mindset.

The unfortunate consequences of the situation fell upon the criminals' family members that resided in the area. Although no one in the community harbored resentment toward them, it put them in a difficult position. The police had been in contact with many of them and had certain members and households under surveillance. Still, no one was considered guilty by association by either law enforcement or the general public. Family members tried to go about their daily lives the best they could. Fortunately, the criminals' children were young enough so that they could not comprehend what was transpiring. Still, they undoubtedly would have to carry with them and navigate the crimes for the rest of their lives.

Batley, the only criminal still in the area, was hiding at his girlfriend's house and telling anyone who would listen about the crimes. That was how many of the rumors initially began. He told others that Perrine, McConnell, and Hosack were in big trouble but continually downplayed his role in the crimes. By late afternoon, several calls had come into the police station from people claiming to have pertinent information regarding the investigation. Most of the claims involved second- and third-hand information that ultimately was traced back to Batley. Everything was recorded, logged, and followed up on, but the immediate concern was finding Mike because everyone believed him still alive.

As the rumors continued to grow with every telling, they were bolstered by more exaggeration. Everyone seemed to have a small piece of inside information about the criminals or the crimes, but at this point, everything was complete speculation or fabrication. Law enforcement worked diligently to separate fact from fiction and feverishly attempted to keep the investigation focused. The entire county was a cesspool of gossip, and local telephone operators struggled to keep party lines open as the news spread throughout the region like wildfire. The only certainty was that a quarter of the borough's current population now consisted of law enforcement. The town was nearly under complete lockdown and would remain that way until Mike was located.

////////////

The police station was a flurry of activity as personnel worked to keep the investigation moving forward. Dispatch was in continuous contact with the officers in the field, coordinating the search for Mike while running down leads on the criminals. The telephones hadn't stopped ringing in hours, and now media outlets from across the state were beginning to query about the crimes, with surrounding community leaders requesting updates. Local law enforcement asked for additional resources from surrounding state agencies to avoid a public relations disaster, and the FBI also became active in the investigation. It appeared that no one would be going home in the foreseeable future, and then the unimaginable happened.

At precisely 9:23 p.m., the police station doors swung open, and nineteen-year-old Gary Lee Batley walked in, accompanied by his mother and his girlfriend's mother. As if a great vacuum had sucked the air out of the room, you could hear a pin drop as everyone focused on the main entrance. Three officers quickly escorted the trio into an office and closed the door behind them. Batley's mother stated, "He wants to turn himself in."

One of the officers read him his rights and another asked him to repeat them back and then asked if he fully understood them. Batley claimed he did, saying, "I just want to get my part in the matter cleared up." His mother pleaded with him to get a lawyer before making a statement, but he refused.

The first thing Batley said was, "The big guy's up Skunk Lane, back of Bestwick's." The interrogation immediately ceased only minutes after it had begun. That was all the information the officers needed to pinpoint Mike's location, and believing he was still alive, the call went out for all law enforcement in the immediate area of Jackson Center to meet at the Winklevoss garage as soon as possible. Batley was then placed in a patrol car, accompanied by three officers, and rushed to Jackson Center.

Jean and Kathy arrived in different vehicles at the rendezvous spot but were immediately placed in the back seat of the same patrol car. At nearly 10:00 p.m., six police cars and twice as many officers were currently in the parking lot. Uncertain of what was happening, the girls sat quietly in the car with two officers as a seventh police car approached. As the arriving patrol car pulled in next to them, one of the officers in the front seat told them to keep their heads down. For the first time in over twelve hours, the girls saw Batley sitting in the back of the arriving patrol car.

Skunk Lane was less than two miles from their current location, so the car containing Batley pulled out in the lead, with Jean and Kathy's car next and the remaining five police cars following behind. As they turned into Skunk Lane, Jean immediately recognized the white house that was later determined to be the Bestwick residence. As the lane curved, Kathy pointed out and identified the piece of machinery she remembered from the previous evening and excitedly said, "This is where we were parked." Finally, they had found where Mike had been taken from the trunk.

One officer was left to stand guard outside of Batley's car, and another officer was posted at Jean and Kathy's car while the rest proceeded up the lane. Walking slowly, the officers observed three sets of footprints in the mud heading in the same direction they were walking. They followed the tracks for approximately one hundred feet before losing them at the coal yard's edge. At this point, the officers fanned out with their flashlights and slowly moved forward. Having only gone a short distance, an officer called out that he'd found something.

The first evidence discovered was a half-full can of Black Label beer sitting upright. Next, a cigarette butt was found a few feet from the beer can, along with a spent .22-caliber shell casing. Further inspection revealed freshly moved earth, so a shovel was called for and produced. After three shovelfuls of coal dust were removed by Trooper Ralph Lettieri, a pair of blue denim jeans were revealed, and it was quite apparent to everyone on the scene that they were looking at a person's leg. The officers then took turns meticulously unearthing the rest of Mike's body while taking photographs as they progressed. Mike's glasses were found buried next to him and were carefully removed along with his body and laid next to the shallow grave.

A detail of officers was left to preserve the crime scene as generator-powered flood lights, the district attorney, and the county coroner were called in. Four of the police cars and half of the officers, along with Batley, Jean, and Kathy, returned to the police station. At 10:50 p.m. on March 29, nearly twenty-six hours after they'd been abducted, Rick, Jean, and Kathy were sent home with their families. Mike's parents were sequestered in a private room and told the heartbreaking news of Mike's discovery. In the coming hours, Mike's dad would be escorted to the morgue at Bashline Hospital to identify his son. After he was transported to the police station, Gary Lee Batley gave a formal statement concerning the crimes. He was charged with kidnapping and rape and reprimanded to state custody. A murder charge would be added at a later date.

////////////

As the criminals began to stir during the late morning hours of March 30, they had no inkling that a thirteen-county manhunt was underway, and nearly every newspaper across the state had reported on their crimes. Spending one night in the solitude of the cabin was more than enough for them, and they intended to reach out to their new co-conspirator to help them formulate a plan to get out of the state. Driving several miles farther east, they located a pay phone near a campground shortly after 12:00 p.m. The news they received from back home was completely unexpected.

In less than thirty-six hours, law enforcement knew their identities, had searched McConnell's residence, knew the type of vehicle they were driving, and had discovered the body of the person they'd killed and buried. They were also informed of the significant police presence throughout Mercer County, and that the attitude of the locals was to shoot them on sight. The most recent rumor was that Batley had surrendered and given the rest of them up. With panic setting in, the conspirators formulated a plan for all parties to meet up later that night to get rid of the blue Ford. The criminals then returned to the cabin and waited until well after dark, at which point they unbelievably drove right back into the heart of the manhunt to meet with the only friend they had.

Successfully avoiding law enforcement, the criminals reentered Mercer County during the early morning hours of March 31 and met up with their co-conspirator at a strip mine off State Route 258 near Blacktown. After removing their firearms from the vehicle, they rolled down the windows, placed it in neutral, and then pushed the blue Ford down the embankment into the water. Watching from above until the car was completely submerged, their accomplice drove them to a farmhouse near the Amish community of Volant to hide out.

The following day, April 1, Mercer County State Police received an anonymous tip claiming thirty-five-year-old Harry Barnes, Sr. was assisting the wanted criminals to escape capture. They were currently hiding at a farmhouse in Lawrence County. Immediately responding to the tip, six troopers were dispatched to investigate this new lead. As the patrol units pulled into the driveway, they surprised Barnes and Hosack, who were loitering outside. Barnes ran towards an outbuilding while Hosack, who was armed, attempted to run to the house. Commanded to halt and drop his weapon, Hosack raised his rifle at an officer and was promptly shot in the back and buttocks by another officer. Barnes was unarmed and apprehended, hiding inside the outbuilding.

The officers quickly surrounded the farmhouse and told its occupants to surrender. Opening an upstairs window, Perrine yelled, "Don't shoot! We surrender, we surrender!" He and McConnell threw their weapons out the second-story window then exited the farmhouse and presented themselves to the officers. Perrine, McConnell, and Barnes were taken into police custody, and Hosack was taken by ambulance to the hospital, where he would survive his wounds. Four days after it had begun, the second largest manhunt in the history of the state was over.

///////////

As the criminals were searched, read their rights, placed in separate patrol cars, and shuttled away, additional units and crime scene investigators were called to the scene. The items seized from the criminals included a single-shot 12-gauge shotgun loaded with slugs, a 20-gauge pump shotgun loaded with slugs, a loaded .22-caliber Winchester rifle, a man's sock containing sixty-five rounds of .22-caliber ammunition, a straight razor, Bugler smoking tobacco, three packs of Marlboro cigarettes, a flashlight, seventy-five cents, and the Speidel-banded Benrus wristwatch that was removed from Perrine's wrist.

As Perrine was transported back to the Mercer County State Police barracks, he began talking and wouldn't stop. He was again advised of his rights and told to remain quiet until an attorney was appointed to him, but he no longer displayed a tough-guy facade; he babbled nonstop about the crimes after his capture. He discussed everyone's roles in the crimes and stated that Hosack was the shooter. He claimed, "The first night we spent in the woods, and the next day we came to Harry Barnes because we needed money." Perrine then told them where they'd dumped the blue Ford and that Barnes was hiding them until he could smuggle them out of the state. His unsolicited statements were documented, and plans were immediately set in motion to retrieve the blue Ford.

The following day, April 2, the State Police found what they believed to be the strip mine Perrine had described and where the blue Ford was submerged. After thoroughly searching the area, they found tire tracks where a vehicle had entered the water. Arrangements were made with the State Police scuba team to search the strip mine. The following day, scuba team officers Newton Robbins and Elmer Beaver confirmed that the blue 1968 Ford with registration 3A3 222 was submerged in the water. A towing service was contacted, and the blue Ford was extracted from the water and taken into police custody.

Documentation noted that the vehicle was in neutral, with all its windows down, headlights in the on position, and the trunk key in the trunk lock. No fingerprints could be lifted from the car due to its submersion. Further investigation revealed an unspent .22-caliber cartridge underneath the rear seat, and behind the back seat, an empty box of .22-caliber Remington shells was located. In the trunk of the car, above the right rear wheel housing, eighteen unspent .22-caliber cartridges were found along with a large button bearing the words "J.C. Higgins." The final two items the search of the blue Ford uncovered were found in the glove box: two pieces of mail, one addressed to Gary L. Batley R.D. #2 Jackson Center, and another addressed to his mother.

Events proceeded rapidly, and Kenny Perrine, Arthur McConnell, Donald Hosack, and Gary Batley were all charged with murder, voluntary manslaughter, burglary, larceny, and rape. All four were held over without bond, and a preliminary hearing was set for June 3, 1968. All four defendants pleaded not guilty. Co-conspirator Harry Barnes was charged and sentenced separately with aiding and abetting.

Once he was taken into custody, Perrine continually changed his story, perjured himself during the Barnes trial, and changed his guilty plea to not guilty and then back again. His antics were more of a hindrance than a help to his defense. Many suspected they were an attempt to avoid the death penalty, but they had no bearing on his sentence. Finally, suffering enough of the nonsense, the judge shut his defense down with this statement: "The time for tinkering with the trial court is terminated. Perrine is an admitted perjurer, a man who speaks with forked tongue, a man who, beyond all doubt whatsoever, calmly and nonchalantly was responsible for the death of Kenneth Michael Frick and buried Frick when he was still viable. We cannot escape the reflection that Andersonville would have been an appropriate place to lodge this killer-perjurer. Let him repose in peace at the penitentiary."

Kenneth Eugene Perrine was sentenced to two twenty- to forty-year concurrent sentences for the crimes, plus life without the possibility of parole for Mike's murder.

Arthur Paul McConnell was sentenced to two twenty- to forty-year concurrent sentences for the crimes, plus life with the possibility of parole for Mike's murder.

Donald Russel Hosack was sentenced to two twenty- to forty-year concurrent sentences for the crimes, plus life without the possibility of parole for Mike's murder.

Gary Lee Batley was sentenced to two twenty- to forty-year concurrent sentences for the crimes, plus life without the possibility of parole for Mike's murder.

6

STATEMENTS AND DOCUMENTS

On March 29, 1968, Rick, Jean, and Kathy gave their initial statements about the events that had transpired until their rescue earlier that morning. The coeds had endured hours of horrific and merciless treatment from their abductors and had differing perspectives on the timelines and events. Only after perusing over 800 court documents and the testimonies from both the victims and perpetrators could an accurate timeline and course of events be established. These events are laid out in the previous chapters in much greater detail. Following are the coeds' statements as they were recorded on the day of their rescue.

Rick's Statement 3/29/1968

"We were abducted at about 10:00 or 10:30. Frick and I were put in the trunk of the car, and the girls were put in the front. We drove around until 11:00 or 11:30, then the car stopped. I was asked to get out and learn a few boxing lessons. I was smacked around a couple of times and put back in the trunk. We could hear them abusing the girls, and we took off again about 2:00. They drove around about half an hour, and the car stopped. They asked us if we had enough air, and Frick said no. They told him to quit getting smart. After driving around some more, they stopped and opened the trunk, and told Frick to get out. He got out about half an hour later; they came back, put shovels in the trunk, and took off. Drove around again, they took shovels out of the car, were arguing, and put shovels back in the trunk. Drove around for about 15 minutes then the car stopped. Something was wrong with the car. Two guys left, two guys stayed; they came back with another car around 4:00, did some work on the car, and took off. Drove around until we stopped at a house. They took the girls in first, then came out, opened the trunk, I got out, put my hands behind my back, they tied them, then moved me into the house. I was taken upstairs, told to lie face down on the bed; they tied my hands to my feet and neck and said if anyone came and I talked, I would die. I stayed tied up until about 8:00. A man came to the house in a white and red car, 68. He stopped and knocked on the door, but no one answered. Kathy came upstairs with Gary. I heard Jean scream. Don was trying to grab her. Ken and Art went somewhere. Don was supposed to stay back and watch us. Gary gave me a knife. We waited about half an hour, and when Don wasn't looking,

Kathy, Jean, and I tried to jump Don. Kathy threw pop in his face, Jean took his gun, and I stabbed him. Then we pushed him down and ran down the stairs and up over the fields behind the house until we came to a house with a phone and called the state police."

Jean's Statement 3/29/1968

"On March 28 at approximately 9:30 p.m., four men, whose names we learned to be Gary, Ken, Art, and Don as they referred to each other, approached the car I was in with Rick, Kathy, and Mike, parked at the Coat of Arms. They each had rifles, summoned the boys out of the car, frisked and took their wallets, then made them get into the trunk of their car, a blue Ford. Kathy got in the front, I got in the back, each of us between two guys. They drove towards Mercer and went back along some railroad tracks. We were here from about 10:40 to 12:30, and Kathy and I were raped by each. From here, we went to some sort of storage place, which they broke into and stole two shovels. Then we drove for only a short time, turned at a white house, went back a road, and stopped. Ken and Art left with the two shovels for about half an hour, then came back, and Ken and Don took Mike out behind the car where I couldn't see him. During this time, Kathy and I were raped again by Art and Gary. The other two came back after about 15 minutes without Mike. I figured this to be around 1:00 a.m.

From there, we drove a short distance and stopped. Gary and Art took the shovels to the top of a hill. They were gone about 15 minutes. When they returned, they were sort of quarreling about someone being a chicken or something. We left and drove for a while and ended up stranded on a dirt road by Gary's house because the car broke down. Ken and Art left to get another car. It seemed like they were gone for ages because Kathy and I were raped the entire time by Don and Gary. We were there until about 4:00 a.m. Ken and Art came back with the other car. It was a dark Galaxie license number R09-392. They worked on the other car for a long time and got it in running order again. From there, we drove around some more. Kathy and Ken in the Galaxie, and the rest of us, including Rick, still in the trunk, in the blue Ford. We raced around for a while until we got stuck but then went to Gary's house, where Ken got rid of the Galaxie and got in with us. Finally, around 5:30, we went to this cabin which Art had the key. I slept on the couch with Don. Kathy was in the bedroom with Ken, where she was raped again, and Rick and Gary were upstairs. Now all night, Gary kept telling us he was going to help us get away. So when Ken and Art left about 9:30 a.m., he decided we should jump Don and take off. We sat around waiting, and he took Kathy in the bedroom and raped her again, and then went upstairs. Don tried to rape me again, but I refused and ran up the stairs where Kathy, Rick, and Gary were. Gary slipped Rick a knife. About 10:15 or so, Gary went downstairs, and we never saw him again. About 10:30, I grabbed Don's gun from his hands, Kathy threw 7UP in his eyes and started pounding him with the mug, and Rick stabbed him in the stomach. Then we took off. He grabbed Kathy, but she broke loose, and we ran up behind the house. I turned and saw Ken and Art pulling in, and the next time I looked, I saw Don pointing a gun in our direction. Apparently, he never fired it, though. We ran up over the hill, through bushes, cornfields, barbed wire fences, and phoned the police at the nearest house."

Kathy's Statement 3/29/1968

"On the 28th of March, about 9:30 p.m., four men who called themselves Gary, Art, Don, and Ken ordered Jean, Rick, Mike, and myself from our car, which was parked in front of the Coat of Arms. After they took Mike and Rick's wallets, they put them in their trunk, and Jean and I up in the front with them. We headed for Mercer, and about 10:40, they pulled off an old dirt road and proceeded to rape both Jean and I. All four took their turns with both of us. About 12:30 a.m., we left the railroad tracks and headed up to a storage box along the road. They broke into it and stole two shovels, which they put in the backseat. After what seemed only like 10 minutes, they pulled into another dirt road, which led to a muddy area. They parked the car facing the main road, and Ken and Art took the shovels, walked behind the car, and didn't return for approximately 30 minutes. When they came back, they took Mike out of the trunk. Jean and I were raped again. We then drove around and ended up on a dirt road just down from where Gary lives. The car broke, and Ken and Art decided to get another car. Jean and I were raped again. This all happened between 2:30 a.m. and 4:00 a.m. Ken and Art came back with Ken's car and fixed the one we were in. We went for a ride around all the back roads. Jean and I were in separate cars. After that, Ken took his old car home, and we all rode in the same car. In about 10 minutes, we were at the old house that Art had a key for. They told Jean and I to go lay down for a while, and they took Rick upstairs. They said we could go to sleep, but they raped us again first. In the morning, Gary told us two guys would be leaving soon, and we'd have our chance to escape then. I went upstairs with Rick, whose hands were untied, and Gary came up, too. Art and Ken Finally left, and Jean came upstairs. At 10:15, Gary went downstairs and never came back. Jean made a grab for the gun; I threw pop in his face and hit him with the mug. Rick stabbed him in the stomach. We ran down the stairs and out of the house. Jean had his loaded gun. When we were in the middle of the first field, we turned around and saw Don standing, aiming his rifle at us. We ran across the fields and phoned the police from one of the houses along the road."

///////////

Gary Lee Batley's Interrogation 3/29/1968

After leading police to the location of Mike's body on March 29, 1968, Gary Lee Batley was transported back to the Mercer County State Police barracks, where he gave his version of the crimes. He refused his right to legal counsel and willingly answered all questions. At the conclusion, he was charged with kidnapping and rape and reprimanded to state custody. A murder charge would be added at a later date. Lieutenant Rice, Corporal Molzan, and Trooper Mifsud of the Pennsylvania State Police conducted the following interrogation.

Q. Alright Mr. Batley will you start in your own words and tell us about your own activities on Thursday night which would be March 28, 1968.
A. Well, I was down at the gas station with my buddy and my brother pulled in and asked me, he said, "Do you want to go drink a few beers?" I said, "Yeah."

Q. Now, when you say your brother, who do you mean?
A. Ken.

Q. Ken who?
A. Perrine

Q. Ken Perrine – Kenneth Perrine – P-e-r-r-i-n-e?
A. Yes, sir. And I said, "Yeah." We go down and this Donnie Hosack said he knows where there's this nice place to drink some beer.

Q. Now, may I interrupt you here? You say your brother, Kenny Perrine, asked you to go get some beer and you got in the automobile? Whose automobile was this?
A. It was a rented car from Robbins.

Q. Who was in the automobile when you got in?
A. Art - Art McConnell, my brother, Ken Perrine, and Donnie Hosack.

Q. Now, where does Donnie Hosack live?
A. Nowhere.

Q. Where does Art McConnell live?
A. Out at – on Oakland Road.

Q. Alright now, you started down the road going to get a drink of beer. Now, you take it from here.
A. Donnie took us out to this place – I don't know where it was at – out by Slippery Rock. These kids was there – two girls and two boys – and my brother Ken says, "Let's get them in the car." So, Donnie Hosack and my brother, Ken, and Art McConnell – they all got out of the car and walked over to the car and told them all to get out. They all got out of the car, and they told them they was going to go for a ride with us in our car, and my brother, Ken, put the two boys in the trunk, and the two girls inside the car. Then from there we went to Bestwick's.

Q. Bestwick's? Where is that located?

A. Skunk Lane. That's in Jackson Center.

Q. Alright. Continue...

A. We went up there to a little place and my brother, Ken, and Art McConnell had a couple of shovels they took out. They went back in the strip mine and dug a hole. Then they come back and Donnie, and my brother Ken, went out and took one boy out of the trunk of the car and they shot him back there and buried him. Then we went from there past my house on 62. We was going back another dirt road and the car broke down. Art and Ken walked to my house. His wife come out and they went up and fixed the car. Then we went from there out to Art McConnell's house. We stayed there overnight. In the morning my brother, Ken, and Art left and Donnie Hosack was there with the four, or the three of us – count me out as four. Then I told Donnie I was going out for some fresh air, and I run out through the field and came into Mercer here and I went to Mrs. Walter's house to get cleaned up and then we went to the hospital and then from the hospital we went to the gas station and then from the gas station we went to my sister's house and then from there we come down to the police barracks.

Q. Alright now, the car that you went down toward Slippery Rock in – the four of you, Art McConnell, Donnie Hosack, and Kenny Perrine, your brother – what type of automobile was this?

A. 68 Ford.

Q. And what was the color of this automobile?
A. Blue.

Q. Who drove it to the place you speak of in Slippery Rock?
A. My brother.

Q. Kenny Perrine?
A. Yes, sir.

Q. Now, in this restaurant at Slippery Rock where you pulled in, was this place open for business?
A. I don't think so.

Q. Were there lights around the place or was it dark?
A. It was dark.

Q. Do you know what time you arrived there?
A. It must've been right around 11:00 or 11:30.

Q. Now, when you pulled in you say you saw two fellows and two girls?
A. Yes, sir.

Q. Where were they when you saw them?
A. Sitting in the car drinking beer.

Q. What kind of car were they sitting in?
A. 60 Chevy station wagon.

Q. And did you notice who was sitting in the front seat and who was sitting in the back?
A. No, sir.

Q. In other words, were both boys in the front and both girls in the back, or one each?
A. There was one each.

Q. Now you said someone got out of your automobile, the 68 Ford. Who got out of that automobile?
A. My brother, Ken, and Donnie Hosack, and Art.

Q. And what did you do?
A. They told me to get out too.

Q. Now, when you say they went over to the automobile did they have a gun, arms, or anything?
A. Yes, sir.

Q. Who had the guns and what type of guns were they?
A. Two of them had – my brother, Ken, had a .22 rifle, Donnie Hosack had a .22 rifle, and Art McConnell had a 20-gauge pump.

Q. All three of them had guns, then?
A. Yes, sir.

Q. What did they do next when they saw these boys and a girl?
A. They told them all to get out of the car.

Q. And what did they do once they were all out of the car?
A. My brother told them to get into the trunk. The two of them was going for a ride – the two boys got in the trunk.

Q. And they got in the trunk?
A. Yes, sir.

Q. Now was anything taken from these two boys when they got out of the automobile?
A. I don't know, sir. I wasn't watching.

Q. Now, the two boys were put into the trunk. Is that correct?
A. Yes, sir.

Q. Who ordered them into the trunk?
A. My brother.

Q. Kenny Perrine?
A. Yes, sir.

Q. And what were the other two men doing – McConnell, and what was the other lad's name?
A. Donnie Hosack.

Q. Yes. Hosack. What were they doing when your brother, Perrine, was putting them in the trunk?
A. Watching the girls so they didn't run away.

Q. And what happened to the girls? Where were they put?
A. They was put inside the car.

Q. Front seat – back seat – or where?
A. One was put in the front seat and one was put in the back seat.

Q. Now, who rode in the car when you left there—of you men—there was one girl in the front seat and one girl in the back seat, right?
A. Yes, sir.

Q. Now, who was in the front seat with one girl?
A. My brother, Ken, and I.

Q. Who was in the back seat with the other girl?
A. Art McConnell and Donnie Hosack.

Q. Now you pulled out of there and drove to where?
A. Bestwick's.

Q. And that's in Jackson Center?
A. Yes, sir.

Q. Now, did you stop between Slippery Rock and Bestwick's?
A. Just one time. To turn around. We missed a road.

Q. They missed the road?
A. Yes, sir.

Q. And you just turned around there and went over to Jackson Center? What did you do there in Jackson Center?
A. My brother, Ken, got out of the car – he told Art to come with him. They got two shovels out of the trunk. Then they shut the

trunk back up and they walked out through the woods. Then they come back and put the shovels in the trunk and told the boy to get out of the trunk. Then Art got back in the car and Donnie Hosack and my brother, Ken, walked into the woods with the boy.

Q. Which boy did they walk back with? Do you know them?
A. No, sir.

Q. Do you know them by description?
A. One was real big.

Q. Do you know the one that went back? What color of hair he had?
A. No, sir.

Q. Well, now between the time you left Slippery Rock with these girls, and the boys in the trunk, didn't you stop someplace to molest the girls?
A. Yea. We stopped out along Dump Road.

Q. And what did you do when you stopped there?
A. My brother, Ken, and Donnie Hosack walked down the railroad tracks with the girls.

Q. And what did you do?
A. I sat in the car.

Q. And what did Art McConnell do?
A. He sat in the car too, sir.

Q. And it was during this time the boys were still in the trunk?
A. Yes, sir.

Q. Now, getting back to where we left off, where they walked into the woods, these two men walked into the woods, that was Kenny Perrine and who?
A. Donnie Hosack.

Q. Yes. Donnie Hosack. They walked into the woods with two shovels?
A. That was Art McConnell and my brother, Ken. Ken Perrine who walked into the woods with shovels, sir.

Q. Now to get this straight, Art McConnell and who walked into the woods with shovels?
A. Ken Perrine.

Q. Yes. Ken Perrine. And when they came back, they put the shovels in the trunk?
A. Yes, sir.

Q. And there was one boy still in the trunk?
A. They was both in the trunk and then my brother, Ken, told the big one to get out of the trunk. He got out and my brother, Ken, and Donnie Hosack walked back into the woods with him.

Q. Are we clear on this now? Who went back into the woods? The two who walked this college boy back into the woods?
A. Donnie Hosack and Ken Perrine.

Q. And when they came back, the college boy wasn't with them?
A. That's right, sir.

Q. Would you describe this location where the car was sitting when this boy went back in the woods with these two men?
A. It was sitting up by Bestwick's. Skunk Lane where the trucks been traveling to haul coal out.

Q. And is this near Jackson Center?
A. Yes, sir.

Q. And you knew this strip mine out there belongs to Bestwick's?
A. I don't know whether it belongs to him or not.

Q. It's in the vicinity where he lives?
A. Yes, sir.

Q. And have you been back to this same spot since?
A. Yes, sir. Tonight.

Q. And were you with State Police officers when you went back there tonight?
A. Yes, sir.

Q. And that is the same place where you saw the two men go into the woods with the boy and come out without him?
A. Yes, sir.

Q. What happened next?

A. Then we went from right there and the car broke down. My brother, Ken, and Art McConnell walked down to my house. I am pretty sure that is where they walked to and he must've called his wife, or something and she come out and they went up and fixed the new car and then they took off from there and went to Art McConnell's house and stayed there overnight.

Q. Now when the car was broken down and these two men left who stayed with the automobile?
A. Me and Donnie Hosack.

Q. And where were the two girls during this time?
A. I was in the front seat with one girl and Donnie Hosack was in the back with the other.

Q. And where was the boy?
A. He was still in the trunk.

Q. One boy was still in the trunk?
A. Yes, sir.

Q. Now, you went then to Art McConnell's, right?
A. Yes, sir.

Q. What did you do there?
A. My brother, Ken, tied the boy that was in the trunk – he tied him up, then put him upstairs in Art McConnell's house. My brother, Ken, told me to watch him so he didn't get away – so I went upstairs to watch him. Just me and this boy. I don't know

what was going on downstairs because I wasn't there. Then I went downstairs for a while and fell asleep in a chair. When I went back up the stairs, the boy was untied. He untied himself. He was just setting on the edge of the bed. I said I'll let you untied. I don't want to see nobody else hurt. Then I told him I would help him out. Then come morning someone knocked on the door and my brother, Ken wouldn't let no one answer it. Then my brother, Ken, and Art took a ride somewhere. I don't know where they went. Then I told Donnie I was going outside, and then I run through the woods to Mercer.

Q. Well, now the four of you and the two girls and the boy went into McConnell's house?
A. Yes, sir.

Q. The boy went upstairs, and you were sent up to watch him?
A. Yes, sir.

Q. And the two girls were downstairs with the other three men?
A. Yes, sir.

Q. And then – who left first?
A. My brother, Ken and Art McConnell.

Q. Now, during the time you were riding along had you had any conversation with these men from the time they left with the shovels and this boy? Was there any conversation among these men about what had happened to the boy?

A. Nobody said nothing and then my brother, Ken, told me they shot him.

Q. Your brother, Ken, told you who had shot him?
A. Donnie Hosack.

Q. Donnie Hosack had shot the boy?
A. Yes, sir.

Q. Did they say what they did with him after they shot him?
A. They said they buried him.

Q. Now you left. As soon as you could get away, you ran away?
A. Yes, sir.

Q. Now during the time that you were guarding the college boy upstairs did you furnish him with anything?
A. Yes, sir. I gave him a knife so he could help himself out.

Q. Why did you do this?
A. Because I didn't want to see nobody else hurt, sir.

Q. What was your reason to think they might get hurt?
A. Because I heard my brother, Ken, Art and Donnie talking.

Q. And what did they say?
A. They said they was going to get rid of them too.

Q. And where were you when you heard this conversation?
A. I was in the house.

Q. And where were the girls when this conversation took place?
A. They was sleeping.

Q. Where were they sleeping?
A. One was in the bedroom and one was on the couch.

Q. Now, during the night, at any time, did anyone have intercourse with these two girls?
A. No. Just out along the road. My brother, Ken, and Art McConnell and Donnie Hosack.

Q. Just those three men?
A. Yes, sir.

Q. Do you know which man had intercourse with which girl?
A. They took turns, sir.

Q. And how many times did they have intercourse with these girls?
A. I don't know, sir.

Q. Was it more than once?
A. Yes, sir.

Q. As many as two, three, four times?
A. I don't know, sir. I didn't bother to pay no attention to them.

Q. Where did these fellows get the two shovels? Do you know?
A. Yes, sir. They broke into a state highway box where they keep tools.

Q. A tool shed?
A. Yes, sir.

Q. Do you know where this is located?
A. Out past Dick Johnson's house, going on 62, you make a left by Dick Johnson's,

Q. And was that all they took – two shovels?
A. Yes, sir.

Q. Where did they put the shovels when they brought them to the car?
A. The first time when they brought them to the car, they put them in the back seat. Then they moved them from the back seat and put them in the trunk.

Q. Gary, at Dump Road did you have relations with the girls?
A. Yes, sir.

Q. Both girls?
A. Yes, sir.

Q. You had intercourse with both of them on Dump Road?
A. Yes, sir.

Q. Did you have intercourse with either of the girls at Art McConnell's house?
A. In the morning, sir.

Q. In the morning you had intercourse with one of the girls in the house?
A. Yes, sir.

Q. Do you recall which one?
A. The brown-haired one, sir.

Q. You don't know either of their names?
A. No, sir.

Q. Gary, why did you pull in the other strip mine?
A. I can't think. It's out by Parker's beer garden.

Q. Would that be the Jackson Center – Grove City Road?
A. Yes, sir.

Q. Would that be above or below the Coolspring Church?
A. Above. Towards Jackson Center.

Q. You mean, North?
A. Yes, sir.

Q. What did you do at that strip mine, Gary?
A. Art McConnell and I got out of the car. He walked back and started digging. He told me to dig. I said, "I ain't digging." He called me a chicken. I said, "I ain't going to shoot nobody." He said, "Well let's go then."

Q. Was there a plan formulated to shoot somebody?
A. Art McConnell. I think he was wanting to shoot somebody.

Q. Well who was he going to shoot?
A. I don't know.

Q. Gary, is there anything further that you'd like to say?
A. Just that my brother, Ken, had a watch he took off the boy.

Q. He took off the boy?
A. Yes, sir.

Q. The boy that we found that was dead?
A. Yes, sir.

Q. Do you know when this watch was taken from him?
A. When they went back in the woods, he came back with the watch on.

Q. Did you see him with any money or any wallet that might have been taken from the boy?
A. He had the boy's wallet. He showed me that he had the boy's wallet.

Q. Where did he show you this watch and this wallet?
A. He told me to get out of the car and walked behind the car and he told me that Donnie Hosack shot the boy and he said, "If you don't believe me, I'll take you back and show you." Then he showed me the boy's watch and wallet.

Q. And what kind of gun did they have when they took him back in the woods?

A. .22 rifles.

Q. Each of them had a .22 rifle?
A. Yes, sir.

Alright, now it's exactly 12:35 a.m. and the date is March 30, and this statement is concluded. We still have present Trooper Mifsud, Corporal Molzan – I'm Lieutenant Rice, and your mother here is with you. This is the conclusion of the statement.

///////////

Autopsy Report 3/29/1968

After Mike's body was removed from the shallow coal-dust-covered grave, it was transported to Bashline Hospital in Grove City, Pennsylvania, where an autopsy was performed. Mike's father was called to the morgue after midnight on March 30 to identify his son. The following is the official autopsy report.

NAME: Kenneth M. Frick, Ford City, PA.

AGE: 21 years of age.

DATE OF DEATH: March 29, 1968.

DATE OF AUTOPSY: March 29, 1968.

LOCATION OF AUTOPSY: Bashline Memorial Hospital.

CORONER: John K. Mohney.

PATHOLOGIST: Frederick J. Raisch M.D.

TROOPERS PRESENT: William Mifsud-Harry Lamberton.

CLINICAL SUMMARY: This body is found in a shallow pit covered with cinders and fully clothed. The clothing on the body at the time of discovery at the site of the pit consists of a sweater with multiple blue stripes and a blue collar. Between the blue stripes are white broader stripes. There is a regulation undershirt on the body and regulation shorts. There are black socks, one on either foot. The pants consist of blue denim with a leather belt and apparently a brass buckle. Within the right front pocket there are car keys and a license No. 600 44F Penna. Marked for the year '66. These keys are arranged on a keyring marked "Your key, O'Brian's Plumbing and Heating, Butler Penna., 284-500 Pat. Pending." There is a piece of metal, with four petal-like projections around the central portions marked "Pocket Screw Driver. Fits Most Screws." on one side and on the opposite side there is a picture of a man flexing his biceps and marked around his feet in a circle "Fourway Pocket Screw Driver." The keys are marked "Yale and Towne Manufacturing Co." on one side and U.S.A. on the other side. The other key is marked on one side with "Milwaukee Briggs and Stratton," and the opposite side of the key is marked "G.M. Knockout, Your Key for Greater Value." In addition, there was a piece of metal marked "Under Guarantee, Postage Guaranteed, Any Mailbox." Labeled "Americans Veterans,

Cincinnati, Ohio. 45206." Lastly, in this same pocket there is a gold ring, at least gold plated, marked G.B. and with an amethyst setting. This ring has an inside circumference of 2 cms. The name of "Frick" is discernible on the inside of the gold band. Attached to his leather belt is a piece of clay. In another pocket there is a handkerchief. The clay, studded with cinders, is 6 x 3.5 x 2 cms. At a level of 5 cms. above the base of the neck in the midline on the posterior surface of the neck or at a level 6 cms. below the external occipital protuberance there is a circular wound not unlike that produced by a bullet, the edges of which are black by reason of powder burns. Centrally it measures approximately 3/16 cms. in diam. This adult body male, with dark hair, with blue irises, with teeth in dental repair, with blood in either nasal cavity, with marked nuchal rigidity, without rigidity of the extremities, with moderate posterior postmortem rigidity, with diminished body heat, without additional evidence of trauma of any part of the body save for the bullet wound portal of entry on the posterior surface of the neck.

CENTRAL NERVOUS SYSTEM: The aperture previously described as a bullet wound on the posterior surface of the neck between occipital protuberance and the base of the neck now is evident on the inner surface of the floor of the left posterior cerebral fossa. There the skeletal muscle protrudes through the aperture with ragged, irregular edges, approximately 1.2 cms in diam. and into the left cerebellum and the pons. In the left cerebellum are two small metal fragments, one 1 mm. in diam. and the other approximately 3mm long and 1 mm. in diam. This bullet track then traverses, after penetrating the posterior wall and floor of the left posterior cerebral fossa, through the cerebellum and pons for a distance of approximately 5 cms, and then traverses into the channel evident on the posterior surface of the left maxillary antrum, and beneath and to the left of the sella turcica. This channel traverses into this dense bone for a distance of 2 cms. Here a bullet, markedly mushroomed, approximately 6 mm. in diam. is found. This mushroomed bullet is found in the posterior wall of the left maxillary antrum. There is no evidence of fractures elsewhere in the skull. There is a marked amount of blood in the spinal fluid. The cervical segment of the spinal cord is torn and hemorrhagic. The cerebral hemispheres are moderately edematous, and the sulci are correspondingly obliterated. The lateral ventricles of the cerebral hemispheres contain a moderate amount of bright red blood. There is no evidence of bullet wounds or any other type of injury in any portion of the head, trunk upper, or lower extremities.

THORAX: The pleural cavities, right and left, are free of fluid and adhesions. The right lung exhibits a smooth, glistening visceral pleura. The parenchyma is dark red and sub-crepitant and moderately edematous. There is blood in the bronchi as well as in the trachea, larynx, oro and nasopharynx. The left lung and left pleural cavity are similar to the same structures on the right. The parenchyma of the left lung is moderately edematous. The bronchioles also contain blood. The branches of the pulmonary veins and pulmonary artery of either lung are similar and are without pathology.

HEART: The pericardial sac contains a small amount of light amber fluid. The pericardium and epicardium are smooth, moist, and glistening. There is a moderate amount of subepicardial fatty tissue. The pulmonic, tricuspid, mitral and aortic valves are not dilated. The leaflets of each valve are thin. The mouth of each coronary artery is patent. The lining of the coronary arteries exhibits no atherosclerosis.

PERITONEAL CAVITY: The diaphragm is intact. The cavity is without fluid, blood, or adhesions.

LIVER: The liver, spleen, kidneys, pancreas, supra renal glands, vertebral column, urinary bladder, prostate, testes, gall bladder, biliary ducts, and vena cava system, the portal systems and the gastrointestinal tract, esophagus, stomach, small bowel, appendix vermiformis, and large bowel: None of these structures exhibit evidence of gross pathology. ALL the tissues have the lowered temperature of the moist ground at the grave in the coal-stripped mine.

ANATOMICAL DIAGNOSIS:

- Penetrating bullet wound of the skull
- Bullet wound laceration of the pons and left cerebellum
- Penetrating bullet wound of the posterior wall of the left maxillary antrum
- Metallic (bullet) fragments in left cerebellum
- Hemorrhagic (explosive pressure) of cervical segment of spinal cord
- Hematomyelia
- Edema of the brain
- Edema of the lungs

The bullet fragments taken from the left cerebellum are given to Trooper Harry W. Lamberton who in the presence of the pathologist placed them in a plastic bag with proper label. Trooper Lamberton also placed a larger bullet fragment measuring 6 mm in diam. in another bag labeled as being found in the posterior wall of the left maxillary antrum. The clothes, likewise, properly labeled by Trooper Lamberton, were placed in plastic bags in my presence. Trooper Lamberton left the morgue at approximately 2:15 a.m., March 30, 1968, with the clothes and bullet fragments properly labeled in his possession.

//////////

Photos

The following selected photos were either captured during the course of the investigation or posted in *The Sharon Herald*.

THE TRUNK OF THE BLUE FORD WHERE MIKE SPENT HIS LAST HOURS

A PENNSYLVANIA STATE POLICE OFFICER SEARCHING FOR CLUES
AT THE MURDER SCENE

THE FORD GALAXIE THAT WAS DELIVERED TO PERRINE AT 3:00 A.M.

EXTRACTION OF THE BLUE FORD FROM THE STRIP MINE WHERE THE CRIMINALS HAD SUBMERGED IT

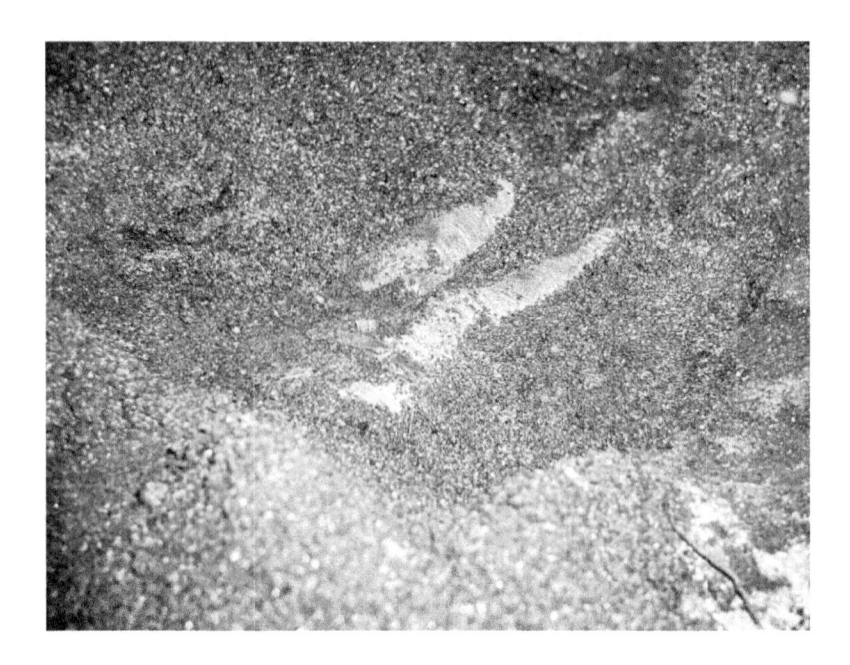

MIKE'S BODY BEING CAREFULLY EXHUMED FROM THE SHALLOW GRAVE

SKUNK LANE

THE MACHINERY KATHY REMEMBERED SEEING WHEN
MIKE WAS TAKEN FROM THE TRUNK

THE UPSTAIRS BEDROOM WHERE THE COEDS JUMPED HOSACK AND MADE
THEIR GETAWAY. KATHY'S 7UP CAN ALONG WITH HOSACK'S BLOOD ARE
STILL VISIBLE ON THE FLOOR

THE TATTERED COUCH WHERE HOSACK SLEPT WITH JEAN

GARY LEE BATLEY BEING LED TO HIS ARRAIGNMENT
(PHOTO CREDIT *THE SHARON HERALD*)

KENNETH EUGENE PERRINE BEING TAKEN TO THE MERCER COUNTY JAIL AFTER HIS CAPTURE (PHOTO CREDIT *THE SHARON HERALD*)

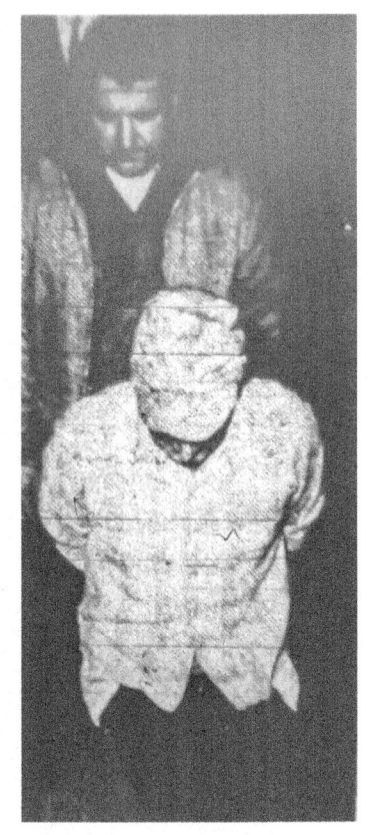

120 *Depravity in the Darkness*

(LEFT) DONALD RUSSEL HOSACK AS HIS PICTURE APPEARED
IN THE NEWSPAPER THE DAY AFTER HIS CAPTURE
(PHOTO CREDIT *THE SHARON HERALD*)

(RIGHT) ARTHUR PAUL MCCONNELL HIDING HIS FACE AS HE'S LED TO JAIL
AFTER HIS CAPTURE (PHOTO CREDIT *THE SHARON HERALD*)

NEWSPAPER HEADLINES AFTER CAPTURE

(PHOTO CREDIT *THE SHARON HERALD*)

Kenneth Michael Frick

The joys and expectations of our First Class year were reduced almost to nothingness by the senseless murder of a Brother Rat. Here was a man who had everything to live for but was cut down by a perverted individual with the sense only to squeeze a trigger. No one gains by such an exchange.

Mike was in the top of the Civil Engineering curriculum and was scheduled to graduate in June with honors. He was known, loved, and respected by all. His easygoing attitude and sound thinking marked him as everyone's friend. But we keep thinking beyond our personal loss to the loss our society suffered at his death.

Statement about Mike's murder put out by
Virginia Military Institute

CONCLUSION

On both sides of these senseless crimes—the victims' and perpetrators'—generations of lives were permanently affected. We are charged with a great responsibility to see that care and conscientiousness be afforded to those who live with the aftermath. For the victims, we recognize with the utmost benevolence and sadness the useless transgressions that were forced upon them. We can never comprehend what they and their families endured as they endeavored to overcome these life-altering events. Undoubtedly, they experienced much pain, sorrow, and suffering, and innocence was forever lost.

I would be remiss to overlook the superb job the Pennsylvania State Police did in solving the case in such a swift and timely manner. Never before, and perhaps never since, has the Mercer County unit been tasked with a crime of this magnitude. Their performance was exemplary—law enforcement at all levels performed above and beyond their call of duty. The only details in the case that avoided discovery were the location where the blue Ford had broken down shortly after the murder and the location of the intended mass grave that had been dug the following morning. All other intricacies relevant to the crimes were uncovered within hours. Even the cabin where the criminals spent their first evening was located, and its owner contacted. Considering the resources available to law enforcement during this time, the police work was remarkable across the board.

While McConnell, Hosack, and Batley realized their destiny in prisons across Pennsylvania until they ceased to exist, fate had something else in store for Perrine. Seven years into his life sentence, he was crushed and cut to pieces in the back of a garbage truck that he willingly climbed into while attempting to escape prison—a merciless end to a troubled young life. We can only hope for all of the meaningless pain and sorrow these four individuals caused during their short existences, that their victims found some solace and justice in the sentences they received for their crimes.

///////////

Made in United States
North Haven, CT
14 July 2023